King of Detroit
The Rising

Written by

Dorian Sykes

RJ Publications, LLC

Newark, New Jersey

The characters and events in this book are fictitious. Any resemblance to actual persons, living or dead is purely coincidental.

RJ Publications

www.rjpublications.com

ISBN-10: 1-939284-01-5

ISBN-13: 978-1-939284-01-3

Printed in the United States

September 2013

1 2 3 4 5 6 7 8 9 10

Dedications

This book is for every nucca that played the game raw, and took his like a man when adversity struck.
And to my co-defendant, Rolo, may we use this time to strengthen our resolve.

Acknowledgements

Ma Dukes- as always, thank you much! Without your steady belief in me none of this would have been possible. From start to finish, Ma', you've held me down and I love you more than life!

Nephews 'RJ' and 'Dee' – May you continue to grow and have a close relationship with God. I love both of you and pray that both of you become a great success. - May ya'll never play this game because it ain't even worth it.

Big Bro Ron, Sr. – What up dough, Lil' Bro making moves man. Thank you, man, for holding down the fort in my long absence, looking after Ma Dukes and being a real father. I truly commend you. Bro, your time is coming.

Linda Huddleston – thank you so much for preparing this book. You've been with me since my first book and it's been nothing short of a pleasure working with you. You really get it done. (Midnight Express Books) – check 'em out!

Unc Gene – What's up man! Nephew making power moves again, baby…

Mojo – I know you're holding it down in the best possible fashion and making noise. We shall cross paths soon my nucca – full embrace. Tell Sha' Boggy I send nothing but luv.

Piwi – Cleveland's finest. What up my dawg. Won't be long now til you touch them streets. You walked it on down like real nuccas do, holla at ya' boy. I won't be too long.

And to the man who made this project possible, COACH – Good lookin' Big Homie for the opportunity. You could have sold your story to a number of big publishing houses, but you kept it gully and I thank you for that. We should do a sequel???

Intro

Interview with Author D. Sykes & Corey "Coach" Townsend

D. Sykes – My man, Coach. How are you?

Coach – I'm blessed, young dawg. How bout you?

D. Sykes – I can't complain. Let's get into it. So, here's the sequel we've all been waiting on. Give the readers a glimpse of what they can expect, and how it's different from part one.

Coach – You know part one, the story was following me through my childhood, I gave the readers a detailed description of how I became the man I am today. In part two, it's me at the top of my game. That's why it's called The Rising.

D. Sykes – So, this is the last chapter. Or can we look forward to a part three?

Coach – there will definitely be a part three to finish off the story. I think we'll call it, The Demise.

D. Sykes – A'ight. Well, do the honors…

Recap

Beep… Beep... Beep... My pager lit up. It was sitting on the coffee table. I raced to pick it up. It read 187, 187, and 187.

I pulled my hoody over my head, cocked my hammer, and then slid out the door. The block was dead. Not a soul was out there. Perfect, I thought, crossing the street like a black cat. Kathy was standing in the half opened door, smoking a cigarette. I climbed the stairs to the house. “Where is he?” I asked, whispering.

“He’s in the bedroom tied up, just like I promised,” advised Kathy, stepping to the side to let me in.

“What about Rocko?”

“They all went clubbin’. And Keith, along with Cane, just left. Besides Dump, I’m the only one here.”

“Good job, here,” I said, handing Kathy a half ounce of crack.

Her eyes lit up at the sight of all the crack. She grabbed the sack and took a seat at the living room table.

I crept toward the back of the house, mag in hand. I peeped through the crack of Dump’s bedroom door. I could see his fat ass all sprawled out across the bed. He was lying on his back. His feet and hands were tied to the head board and base board. I started having flash backs of Dump speaking at King David's funeral, having breakfast with me and Tina, and having me kill Craig… Tears of hate streamed down my face as I pushed the door open and stepped into the room. I stood at the foot of the bed with my 9 mm pointed directly at Dump's sobbing face. I had the trigger about half way pulled, but released it. I wanted his bitch ass to know who was going to kill him. I walked around the side of the bed and slapped the shit out of Dump with the cold steel barrel of my gun. His eyes rolled to the back of his head, and then he came to.

"What the fuck?" he yelled in agony and fear, as he noticed the sheets tied around his ankles and wrists.

I flicked the light on and pulled back my hoody.

"Coach?" asked Dump. 'Boy, what the hell is you doing?" he asked, trying to sit up. "Take this shit off me, right now!" ordered Dump.

"Shut yo' bitch ass up. You ain't runnin' nothin'," I said through clench teeth.

"What is this about, earlier? That shit with you and Rocko?" asked Dump.

"Nah," I said raising my gun to Dump's head. "It's about you and King David," I said.

Dump's eyes locked with the bullet exiting the barrel of my gun. Boom! A long shot rang out, blowing a hole clean through Dump's forehead. His brains flew out the back of his skull painting the wall behind him red.

Boom! Boom! Boom! I put three more shots in Dump's chest just for good measure…

"That's for Craig, bitch!" I yelled furiously at Dump's lifeless corpse. I was steaming. He deserved to die a much worst death. I had let the bitch off too easy, I thought, as I headed out the room…

Chapter One

"Coach, look out!" yelled Eddie.

Boom! Boom! Boom! – Three shots licked off into the night, lighting up the dark street, as Eddie and I exited the Tip and End bar on Mt. Elliot. I ducked low behind the pearl white Seville parked at the curb. Boom! Boom! Two more shots rang out, striking the driver's side of the Caddy bursting the driver's window, then the passenger side where I crunched over trying to pull my .44 bulldog from my pants. Its barrel was too long, that I had to lay flat on my back to pull its nose out. I couldn't tell for sure where the shots were coming from, they just kept coming nonstop.

Boom! Boom! Boom! Boom! - Shots filled the Caddy. Whoever was busting at me knew I was hiding behind the Caddy, and I knew it would be only a matter of seconds before they came and murked me. I took a deep breath and rolled to my knees. "Let's get it," I said rising up gun blazing. Boom! Boom! I let two shots off, while side stepping toward the street. Eddie had pulled the car up.

"Come on, nucca, get in!" Eddie yelled.

I let the .44 pop four more times till it was empty. Boom! I let off my last round as I jumped in the passenger seat and Eddie smashed out. Boom! Boom! Boom! Three shots struck the car as Eddie made a sharp right turn down Robinwood. None of the shots hit me or Eddie.

Feeling like the coast was clear; I sat up in my seat. Eddie hit two corners and was on Nevada heading for the Zone.

"You a'ight, my nucca? You ain't hit, are you?" Eddie asked, looking over at me.

"Nucca, I'm Superman. Superman don't bleed," I said laughing, while gripping the butt of my chrome .44. I was pissy drunk and feeling invincible.

That was the third time in the past week somebody had taken a shot at me, and I'd escaped every last one. The funny thing about it though, I had no clue who was gunning for me.

"We gotta stay outta them damn death traps until we find out who's tryna' hit yo' head," Eddie said, as we pulled in front of my crib on Caldwell.

I knew Eddie was right, but the liquor was talking.

"Man, fuck these bitch ass nuccas. If they want a war, then I'ma give em' one," I said waving my empty gun in the air. 'Nucca, we da mob. Who gon' touch us, huh? Eddie, who gon' touch us?" I asked E, looking him dead in the eyes.

"Nobody," he answered.

"You damn right. We da Goodfellas," I said, as I opened my door and stumbled out of the car.

"Come on, I got you, my nucca," Eddie said, helping me inside the crib.

"Who you calling?" I asked, as I lay on the sofa with my feet kicked up.

"Man, get over here. Somebody just shot at Coach and me as we came out of the Tip and End."

"Word. Who?"

"I don't know. Just get over here. You've seen Nick?"

"Yeah. He's right here."

"Good. Both of ya'll get to the house," Eddie said hanging up the phone.

"Who was that?" I asked half asleep.

"Black. He and Nick are on their way over here. We all need to be together until we can figure this shit out," Eddie said.

"That's right, Captain Kirk. Run yo' ship," I said, laughing.

"Coach, this shit is serious. Somebody is tryna get you out the way, and you sittin' up laughing. Until I can fix this shit, you are not to be out and about. And until I find the nucca tryna kill you and burry his ass, you gotta promise me you're going to chill on that drinking. I need you on point," Eddie said.

"I got you," I said softly, as I drifted off to sleep.

*****

Eddie and I had come to love each other like blood brothers. He was living at the house with me on Caldwell, while Tina was still out in California getting herself together. Eddie was my right hand man and my most trusted out of the crew, which consisted of only four of us. The crew was me, Black, Nick and Eddie. Together we had the city on lock. In the three short months that we had been operating as one, we were now copping 100 bricks of coke twice a week from Nick's dad. Everybody had a role to play, and everybody was getting cake. Whatever I bought for myself, I made sure the whole crew had their own too. And I would pay for it all since I was getting the most money. That's probably why Eddie loved me so much, and was destined to keep me alive.

We all had 500 Coupe Benzos sitting on hammers and decked out with Kenwood sound systems. Nick and Black had the triple black joints, and Eddie and I had the cocaine white ones with the peanut butter guts. I treated everybody to Miami Cuban link 18 karat gold chains with iced out Jesus pieces, and gold presidential Rolex watches. We were shining on them suckas and haters too hard, which is probably why somebody wanted me out of the way. We were stuntin' too hard. We'd pull up four cars deep, hopping out of our 500's with that shit on and the chicks would go crazy. When we hit the bar, nuccas would head for the exit 'cause they knew we came to shut it down. Their little money couldn't be spent when we were in the spot. We bought the bar out every time we hit the club, and our names were starting to ring in the streets. And that's all we really wanted.

We wanted to be hood stars, the youngest and the best who had ever done it...

*****

"Coach, wake up," Black said tapping my leg.

I opened my eyes to see him, Nick and Eddie all seated in the front room.

"What up, dough?" I said sitting up.

"You a'ight, my nucca?" Black asked.

"Yeah, I'm good. You know I ain't bout to let no sucka take me out that easy. Whoever's sending them rookies at me, betta step their game up, if they want my spot," I said.

"You ain't going nowhere, you hear me?" Black said rubbing my head. 'We gon' find these nucca's and put an end to 'em." Black assured.

"Yeah, Coach. We got your back, fool," Nick said.

"And what you gon' do?" I laughed, joking with Nick.

"I'ma bust my gun. Black been taking me to the range to teach me how to shoot and shit," Nick said flashing a brand new Glock.

"Yeah, well you gonna need that, cause it's war soon as we find out who's taking shots at Coach," Eddie said.

"Word, my nucca," Black seconded.

"But until we find this nucca, whoever it is, like I told Coach, he needs to lay low and let us handle all the B.I. and stay outta them hole in the walls," Eddie said.

"Yeah, for real, Coach. Just fall back," Nick said.

"A'ight, I'ma chill for a couple of weeks, but if ya'll don't turn nothing up by then, I'm back doing me. I got nuccas to shine on," I said.

We all busted out laughing and hitting rocks with each other.

Those were my nuccas for real. Right there was the crew, nah, family. Like King David had always told me, "Sometimes in life, a man has to make his own family." Black, Eddie, and Nick were mine…

*****

"What do you mean he got away? Oh you missed, huh? What the fuck were you doing, shooting with yo' eyes closed? I knew I shouldn't have sent yo' rookie ass to do a grown man's job. You might as well not show your face around here no more, either, if you want to keep it." Click. The phone went dead…

"Guess, I'ma have to kill you myself."

Chapter Two

NEW YEAR'S EVE 1994:

It had been a couple of weeks since I stepped out with the crew. I had been laying low like I told the crew I would, while they combed the streets to find out who was trying to kill me. Two weeks, and nothing had turned up. All bets were off. It was New Year's Eve, and there was nothing in the world that could keep me from throwing that shit on.

Black, Nick, Eddie and I were downtown at Broadway's, getting some fresh gear for the party we were throwing that night at the Fox Theatre. Everybody who was somebody was gonna be in the spot and the crew was determined not to be shown up by anybody.

"Teddy, baby," I said as we hit the door to City Slicker's shoe store, right next to Broadway's.

"Coach, my man, what can I do for you today?"

Teddy, one of the sales reps, asked stepping from behind the counter to show the crew some love.

"I need some blocks to match this here," I said, lifting the plastic on my outfit.

"I just got a new pair of Maury's in this morning. They should go great with this. And what about you, white boy Nick? You done been in here damn near everyday this week," Teddy said.

"Since I got my money right, I ain't no gym show nucca no mo'," Nick said.

We all busted out laughing.

Nick had become a local celebrity. Everybody was talking about this white boy who had money. Every time we stepped out, people seemed to know Nick. They'd run up showing him love like "What up, white boy Nick?" He was the center piece to the crew. Black and Eddie weren't on the stuntin' like me and Nick. As long as they had some weed and liquor, they were good. Together, we had become known as the Crew.

Teddy laced all us with Maury gators to match our outfits for the night. One more stop and the look would be complete. We hit up Henry the Hatter on Gratiot and copped some fresh dobs to set the gators off.

"Yeah, that's it," Henry said, as I modeled the hat I picked out. I paid for all our hats, and we stepped out in front of the store.

"Look, I'ma dip out, my nucca. I got some shit I gotta take care of, but I'ma see ya'll tonight at the spot," I said, hitting rocks with the crew.

"A'ight, my dude. Be safe," Eddie said.

We all jumped in our separate cars and peeled off.

*****

It was still early, so I figured I could count out the $3,000,000 for tomorrow's shipment. I handled all the money and inventory of the bricks, that way there would never be any mishaps. I closed all the blinds to the house and made sure all the doors were locked, and then dug up the floor boards in the bedroom of the house. That's where I kept the majority of the money. I pulled the five large trash bags of money out that Black and Eddie had given me over the past two weeks. I dragged the bags into the living room and started running bills through the two money counters sitting on the coffee table.

It took me a few hours to finish wrapping up the money and stashing the remainder. The crew would split that. Counting money always make me tired. I looked at my watch, and I still had a few hours before the party was to start. I kicked back on the sofa and closed my eyes.

*****

Beep! Beep! Beep! The sound of someone's horn woke me up. I looked at my Rolex.

"Damn," I said. I had overslept. It was 11:15.

Beep! Beep! Beep! The horn sounded. I jumped up and ran through the main house and opened the front door. Black, Nick and Eddie were at the curb lined up back to back in their Benzo's. They saw me standing in the door and they jumped out. They had that shit on, and were killin' em'.

"This nucca ain't even ready," Nick said, pointing at my clothes.

"Come in. I'll be ready in a minute," I said, running into the bathroom, and starting the shower. I took a quick five minute shower and dried off.

"Come on, pretty boy. I want to be there when the ball drops!" Black shouted from the living room.

"I'm coming," I said, lacing my gators.

I stood up and checked my situation in the floor mirror. "That be me," I said winking my eyes. I had on a burgundy silk Versace shirt trimmed in gold, with the maroon big block gators with the gold tassels. I was killin' em'. I put my Dob on, cocked it to the side and hit the light. "Let's go shut the city down," I said stepping into the living room.

We all hopped in our Benzo's riding back to back switching lanes. We pulled up in front of the Fox on Woodward Avenue, each of us letting the valet drivers take our keys at the curb. It was 11:40 on the dot, we high-tailed it inside. People waiting to be let in, looked on.

"Who is them nuccas?"

"That's the Crew." I heard some chick say, as I stepped through the golden doors.

My man DJ Ray O'Shay shouted us out as we hit the red carpet where the party was going down at. "The Crew is in the building, ya'll!" Ray shouted through his mic. All the playas and pushas turned and acknowledged our presence.

"White boy Nick," some groupie nucca said pulling up on the set.

"I'ma hit the bar," I said hitting rocks with the Crew, before we broke off…

"Let me get a bottle of Don P," I told the thick lil' white barmaid.

I turned and scanned all that ass up in there. 'Let's see… who's going home with me tonight?" I said to myself. I locked eyes on this chocolate sista. She stood about 5'10", all ass and no titties.

"Here you go," the barmaid said, as she popped the cork on the bottle.

"Thank you," I said. I was about to step away from the bar when ole' girl caught me off guard.
"You know when I first saw the flyer, I told myself that this wasn't you," the barmaid said, then handed me one of the flyers sitting on the bar. The Crew had flicked it up wearing minks and gators. On the flyer it said come party with The Crew on New Year's Eve, and it had our street names beside our picture.
"I said to myself, this can't be the same Coach I met on the greyhound. Not the one who swore he'd call me."
"Jackie?" I said. "Damn, you look different. I didn't even know that was you."
"Mmm. Hm," Jackie uttered.
"What are you doing down here?"
"Some people still have to work for a living, unlike others."
"Come on, give me a break, what can I say, or do to make it up to you?"
"I'm not trippin' for real. It's all good."
"So, besides working, what have you been up to?"
"I'm in school part time, studying to be a nurse."
"That's beautiful...almost as beautiful as you."
"I'm not falling for it this time," Jackie said, blushing.
"Falling for what?" I asked, playing with Jackie's head.
"Stop..." You gon' get me in trouble."

"If I want to flirt with the sexy barmaid, who's gonna stop me? Come on, let's dance," I said, leading Jackie from behind the bar and out onto the dance floor. All the sistas had their murder masks on, as I bumped and grind with Jackie to Color Me Bad's 'I Wanna Sex You Up'. I was all on that soft white ass. Jackie had more ass than just about any other chick in there.

"I see ya', boy," Eddie said. He was grinding with two bucket heads.

The music cut off, and DJ Ray O'Shay announced that the ball would be dropping in 60 seconds.

"So, grab yo' honey dips fellas, and get ready to bring in the New Year with a kiss."

"Ten, nine, eight, seven…" People counted down.

I stood there on the dance floor with Jackie in my arms. I was looking into her eyes, trying to decide if I should kiss her.

"One. Happy New Year!"

I leaned in and kissed Jackie on the lips, just a three second peck, no tongue.

"You didn't have to kiss me, if you didn't want to," Jackie said, as the music turned back on.

"Baby girl, I ain't never in my life, did nothing that I didn't want to do," I said, making Jackie blush again. We were slow dancing to Luther's 'If This World Were Mine…'

"What are you thinking about, Coach?" Jackie asked while looking up into my eyes.

"For once in my life, everything is perfect," I said.

"Well, you deserve it. You've been through so much in your young life. I'm happy for you."

I smiled at Jackie. "Thank you."

Me and The Crew flicked it up in front of this huge Fox Theatre background. We were posted in wooden directors chairs with our legs folded, looking like the young bosses we were. We must've taken a hundred pictures all together. We had hood rats posing in front of us, giving up mean back shots, while we spread money across their backs. It was like a photoshoot. People gathered around us as we did the damn thing.

"That's enough, man," I said, handing the photographer $500.

The party was still jumping, but I was ready to bounce. I had talked Jackie into leaving with me, and my dick was throbbing to get up in that good pussy of hers.

I holla'd at the Crew and told them I was out. They were all parlaying in V.I.P, entertaining the groupies.

"Nucca, it ain't but 1:30," Nick said, looking at his Roly.

"Yeah, Coach. The party is just getting' started," Black said. He was sitting between two yellow bone twins. 'I can't handle both of the PYT's all by myself. We hittin' the Pontchartrain Hotel when we leave here," Black said.

I laughed. "I already got something lined up, but I'm sure you'll be just fine. Take Eddie with you," I said.

"Shit, me and baby girl gon' get a room at the Renaissance," Eddie said. He was all hugged up with the close built chick. All that money my nucca was getting, and his taste in woman still hadn't changed.

"Man, I'm out. Ya'll nuccas be safe. And ya'll know what tomorrow is," I said, hitting rocks with them.

"Let me find out you on white pussy nowadays," Nick teased, as I walked toward Jackie who was serving drinks at the bar.

"You ready?" I asked.

"Yeah, just let me tell my supervisor I'm leaving, and then we can go," Jackie said.

A few moments later, she came walking out the back with her coat on. "We can go now?" she asked.

*****

"Bout time yo' bitch ass got home."

"Ah… shit… That's enough. Wait until we get inside, I said pulling my dick out of Jackie's mouth. She had skulled me up the whole way home.

"Come on," I said, climbing out the car into the brittle cold.

"This your house?" Jackie asked, as we cut across the front lawn from the driveway.

"Yeah," I answered, as I fiddled with my house keys. I stuck the key in the hole and turned the door handle. Soon as the door opened, shots rang out. Boom! Boom! Boom! Boom!

The shots were coming from inside the house. The last thing I saw was flashes of light bursting from the man's gun who was firing shots into my body.

Ahh! Ahh…" I could hear Jackie faintly screaming.

I saw a shadow standing over me, and then a gun raise pointed dead at me.

Boom! Boom! Boom!

"Happy New Year mothafucka'. Bitch, shut the fuck up screaming before I stank yo' ass too."

I could hear footsteps in the distance. It sounded like somebody running…

"Oh, my God. Coach if you can hear me, please don't die on me," Jackie said.

I felt the warmth of her lips touch mine, as she began trying to breathe air into my lungs. She'd breathed into my mouth, and then pumped my chest five times.

"Damn it, Coach. Don't you die on me…"

My entire body went numb. I couldn't feel nothing. I thought to myself, 'I'm fenna die….' I blacked out….

Chapter Three

"Chill out, Black," Nick said, sounding a little scared. Black was going crazy. He was driving like a mad man swerving from lane to lane. "Chill? How the fuck we 'pose to chill when somebody just tried to off Coach?" Black said, switching lanes nearly side swiping an elder white couple.

"All I'm saying is, there ain't no need for us to do nothing' stupid," Nick said.

Black slammed on the brakes, coming to a complete stop. He sat in the middle of Mound Road staring into oncoming traffic. Cars were hitting their horns, and swerving around him. Black reached over the console and grabbed Nick around the collar, then said. "If you scared, you get the fuck out!"

"I ain't scared," said Nick.

"Well, shut the fuck up then," Black said releasing Nick. He pulled back into traffic, and kept into his trans speech. "Somebody round this mothafucka knows something. And its bout to be a lot of flowers bringing and sad singing. We gon' start knocking these nuccas' heads off."

"I'm with that," Eddie said from the back seat.

Black spotted Rome, Ced, and Luke coming out the gas station on 7 Mile and Syracuse. He turned into the station speeding. "And we gon' start with these three bitch ass nuccas," Black said slamming on the brakes.

He damn near hit Ced as the car came to a stop.

"What up Black?" Rome asked, as Nick, Eddie and Black jumped out of the car. Black didn't answer Rome. He had his hands inside the sliding pocket of his hoody.

"I heard what happened to Coach. That's fucked up," Rome said.

"Nah, what's fucked up is this…" Boom! Black put a slug straight through Rome's forehead. He stood over him and finished the job. Boom! Boom! Boom!

"Where the fuck you going?" Eddie asked Ced, as he cut out trying to run. Boom! Boom!

Eddie dropped Ced in his tracks, shooting him twice in the back. "Bitch ass nucca," he said standing over Ced's body. Ced's face was to the ground. Boom! Eddie let off another round into the back of Ced's dome, splattering his brain all over the fresh snow, which decorated the parking lot.

"Kill that nucca!" Blacked ordered.

He was talking to Nick who had Luke at gunpoint. Luke had dropped his soda and chips he had been munching on.

"Please don't kill me," Luke pleaded like a bitch. He just didn't know that Nick was as scared as him. One was scared, and the other one was glad of it.

"Shoot that nucca, and let's go!" yelled Eddie.

Boom! Boom! Boom! Nick let off three rounds into Luke's chest.

Black ran over and put two more slugs in Luke's dome, as he layed sprawled out in the snow leaking like a pig. Boom! Boom! "That's how you finish a mothafucka, now come on," Black said, grabbing Nick by the arm.

They jumped in the car and drove off as if nothing had happened…

Black reached over the console separating him and Nick, grabbing Nick by the collar, he said "Don't you ever hesitate to kill a mothafucka, cause trust me he won't show you the same mercy when you're staring down the barrel at death." Black released Nick's shirt.

Nick's heart was beating so fast, it was damn near about to pop out of his chest.

"Yeah, Nick, the longer you look a man in the eyes before you kill em', the more his ass is going to haunt you. You don't need that shit fucking with your soul. Trust me, I know," Eddie said, firing up another L.

"This is war time. And I need to know that you got my back," Black said holding out his balled up hand.
Nick still a little shaken up, reached out his hand, and hit rocks with Black.
"Coach, needs us. And now ain't the time to be folding," Black said, pulling into the driveway of his crib on Healey. "Come on, let's strap up."
"Here, put these on," Black said, handing Eddie and Nick each bullet proof vests.
"Where you'd you get all this shit?" Nick asked. "You've got enough shit in here to start another world war."
"Yeah, we gon' need it. Cause its bout to heat up round this bitch. Here," Black said, handing Nick a fully automatic SKS with two hundred round drums.
"This is what I'm talking bout," Eddie said, finger fucking the cold steel of his Mack 90. He cocked it back, sliding a .223 round into the chamber.
"Take a few of these," Black said. He was passing Nick and Eddie Army issued colt .45's with the lemon squeeze.
"You bouts to get all the target practice you need," Eddie told Nick.
"Come on, let's ride," Black said.
They switched cars, taking a Buick Le Sabre Black had bought off a crackhead. It was still registered in the custos

name, so he wasn't worried about no heat coming back. This time Eddie was behind the wheel. Black wanted to be the first one out the car when it went down. Nick was sitting low in the backseat with his hoody pulled over his head.

"Pull over right here. That's that nucca Jason off Buffalo," Black said, as Eddie parked behind an old Chevy Celebrity on 7 Mile and Conley at Romel's Beer & Wine store.

"What's up with that fool?" asked Eddie, as they watched Jason walk inside Romel's.

"That bitch ass nucca knows something. And if he don't, he gon' wish he did," Black said, pulling his hoody over his head. In his eyes, anyone's blood was retribution for what happened to Coach. Black knew that somebody knew something, and the more mothafuckas he killed, the more likely he'd kill the nucca who got Coach.

Black's eyes locked in on Jason like a lion on its prey, as Jason exited Romel's. Jason was eating a slice of pizza and playing with his pager, as he walked toward his Cutlas with his head down. He hadn't seen the dark shadows of death emerge from two cars behind. He looked up like a deer caught in headlights. It was too late. Black let his 'K' ride.... Laaka! Laaka! Laaka! Laaka! Black caught Jason twelve times at point blank range before his body even hit the ground.

Lil' Man had bald up on the floor in the passenger side of Jason's cutty. He thought that no one had seen him, but Eddie and Nick were on him. They stood at an angle of each other, and together they aired Lil' Man's ass out. Laaka! Laaka!.... When they finished shooting, Jason's cutty was pierced with rock sized holes and had steam rising out of them. Jason layed slump at the curb with his brains plastered against the bumper of his car.

Black, content with his work, waved Nick and Eddie to come on. "Let's ride, my nuccas."

They jumped in the Le Sabre and got little excited…

"Now, that's how you murk a nucca," Eddie said, reaching in the backseat to give Nick some dap.

*****

"Baby, turn that up. The News 'bout to come on."

"In the wee hours of the morning, this man here, Corey "Coach" Townsend was gunned down at his home on Caldwell Street after leaving a New Year's Eve party downtown at the Fox Theatre. He is listed in critical condition. Doctor's have not yet released a statement of his probability of surviving. And police have not said whether or not anyone is in custody, or if they have any leads.

Again, Corey "Coach" Townsend, known to authorities as a major drug trafficker and head man of 'The Crew', was gunned down. He's now recovering….."

"Cut that shit off! I can't believe this shit. Yo' bitch ass just refuse to die…"

Chapter Four

"Coach, son, get up, you are not going to let this be the end of you. Get up, son. Don't let me down." King David had been coming to me while I was in my coma. "Come on, Coach. Get up," he said.

I opened my eyes and strained from the light. What's all this shit hooked up to me? I thought, as I tried to sit up in bed. "Ahh. Shit!" I yelled.

A sharp pain shot through my entire body and rested in my back. I looked around the room at all the flowers, teddy bears and cards. How long I been in here? I thought, flashing back to the night I had been shot. The last thing I remembered was Jackie trying to give me CPR, which explained why she was asleep in a chair over near the window.

"So, you're awake I see, Mr. Townsend," the doctor said, stepping into the room. 'You've lost a lot of blood, but with proper rest you're going to be just fine," the doctor said, while checking my vitals. "How long have I been here?" I asked.

The conversation woke Jackie up. She smiled from ear to ear as she approached my bed side.

"Almost two weeks," answered the doc.

"Two weeks?" I repeated.

"Yeah, and you can thank this young lady here for keeping you stable until we were able to get you in. She really saved your life. She's going to make a fine nurse one day," the doc said, after finishing his examination.

I looked at Jackie who was now holding my hand. I didn't know how to thank her…

"You've been here with me all this time?" I asked Jackie.

"Everyday around the clock," Doc answered, I'm going to leave you two love birds alone. And you get some rest," Doc said, hitting my feet, then exiting the room.

"How do you feel?" asked Jackie.

"Like shit,"

"You'll get better. I'm here for you, Coach."

"What happened?" I asked.

"All I know is, we were on our way inside your house, and as soon as you opened the door some masked gunmen started shooting…"

My mind was racing. I didn't remember all that.

"Coach, who would want you dead?"

I let out a deep breath, then said "That's a good question? I really don't know."

"Well, whoever it is. It has to be someone who knows you. Otherwise, how'd they get inside your house?"

Jackie was right, I thought. Who the fuck was at my head like that? I wasn't beefing with nobody like that, I told myself… I shrugged my shoulders while staring off into space.

"I don't know," I said.

"Maybe you should move." Jackie said."

"Hell nah," I said. Moving was out of the question. King David had grown up in that house as did I. Caldwell had been in our family for nearly sixty years, I wasn't going anywhere. Plus, I'd feel like I was running, and then whoever was gunning for me would have won.

"Nah, I can't do that," I said.

"What are you going to do?" Jackie said.

I was thinking, but my thoughts were interrupted by the opening of the door. The nurse stuck her head in and said "Sir, you have some visitors here to see you."

Visitors, I thought. Maybe it's Black and the Crew coming to check on me, I told myself. That hope vanished as two older gentlemen wearing trench coats and hats entered the room bearing gold badges. I hadn't been out of my coma ten minutes and these bitches were at my bedside firing questions.

"Mr. Townsend, who tried to kill you?" Detective Noble asked bluntly.

"That's your job to figure that shit out. If you find out, let me know," I said.

"This isn't a game. Somebody wants you dead. What, you don't think we know about the other three recent attempts on your life. Should I tell you how you were nearly killed coming out of the Tippin and End on Mt. Elliot last month?" His partner said, playing good cop/bad cop.

"Listen, I am not interested in your theories, or street gossip some ten dollar snitch told you. But my lawyer might be interested. Give him a call if you have anything further," I said.

"You wanna lay up and play hard ass, when we're here trying to help you. You know what, fuck you. I hope someone does kill your ass. It'll make my job a lot easier. Piece of shit," Detective Noble said, heading for the door with his partner in tow.

"Likewise!" I yelled as they slammed the door.

"They've been in here everyday. They been pressing me for a statement, but I told em' I don't know shit," Jackie said.

"That's good. They can't help me. All they want is a conviction. They don't give a damn how or who they get it on. I damn sure ain't bout to help em'. My justice is gonna be in blood..." I said, getting angrier by the second.

"Calm down, Coach. Your blood pressure is rising," Jackie said. She was caressing my head with her soft hands. "You're going to be okay, Coach. I'm here for you," She said, then kissed the side of my face.

I was in a zone. The only thing on my mind was murder....

Chapter Five

"Hey Black, who is that on the monitor?" asked Eddie. He was referring to the man standing at the door ringing the buzzer to the detail shop. Black had opened up a detail shop on Nevada and Gable, where they did piping for car seats and stereo system installations. The building was surrounded with state of the art security system equipment. Black zoomed in on the man's face, then buzzed him in. "That's Hub Cap."

"What the fuck kind of name is that?" Eddie asked, laughing. He and Black were posted in Black's office getting blunted.

"Black," Hub Cap called out from the front counter.

"Let me see what this fool wants." Black got up and went out front.

"What up, dough Cap? What can I do for you?" Black asked, stepping from behind the counter.

Hub Cap was looking nervous, as Black noticed. "What's up Cap, you a'ight man? You sweatin' like a dope fiend."

"It's Rocko," Hub Cap said.

"What about Rocko?"

"He's tryna' kill me. That's why you ain't been seein' me round lately. He said, he's gone kill me," Hub Cap said, shaking like a leaf.

"What did you do?" Black asked. He knew Cap's history of being a shady nucca, but better yet, Black knew Rocko. Rocko wasn't going to just kill somebody unless that they really deserved it.

"Who else here?" Cap asked, looking around.

"It's all good, ain't nobody back there except my man. Tell me what's up."

"Rocko wants me dead because I got something on him that he doesn't want to get out."

"Like…"

"This is gone fuck you up. I know Coach is ya' man and I got love for the nucca too, which is why I'm tellin' you this."

"What about Coach?" Black said eyes bucked.

"Rocko's the one tryna' kill Coach. Listen, Black, I know you don't believe me, but I'm not lying man, I swear. Rocko hired me to kill Coach, but I kept missing on purpose 'cause I couldn't kill the nucca. I was the one who took shots at Coach coming outta Tippin and End. That was me. You know my aim, I could have easily killed Coach, but I couldn't do it. Now Rocko's tryna' kill me 'cause he doesn't want this to get out. I need your help, Black," Hub Cap pleaded.

"You're not lying to me, are you?" Black asked Cap.

"Black, man, I swear to you. Why would I make this shit up? Rocko's mad because ya'll making all the money in the Zone. The only bread he's touching is outta town. He wants Coach out the way, and you might be next."

"So, what do you want me to do exactly?" asked Black.

"I need somewhere to stay until you know, until you can even things with Rocko. I want to get on the team. You know you and Coach always been my mans, but when ya'll stop fucking with Rocko, it's like ya'll stopped fuckin' with everybody."

"Here's what I'ma do. I'ma put you up, just until I can get Rocko's ass. Then we gon' get this money. Do you know where Rocko's at?"

"I haven't seen him since he threatened to murk me, but I think he's out in Adrian getting money."

"Hey Eddie!" Black called out.

Eddie came walking from behind the counter to where Black and Hub Cap were standing.

"Hub Cap, this my man E-Double. Hub Cap's real good people," Black said introducing the two. 'Look, E, I need for you to do me a solid and drop my man Cap off at the spot on Dean. Lay 'em out nicely for me. He's crew."

Eddie had been listening to the entire conversation. He knew exactly what Black meant by lay em' out nicely. Eddie looked at Hub Cap,

"You ready, playboy?" Eddie asked Cap.

"Yeah. Thank you so much Black, man. I won't forget you," Hub Cap said.

I know you won't, Black thought to himself.

*****

"So, what part of the city you from?" Eddie asked Cap. They were sitting in the drivethru at Miley & Miley's Shrimp Shack.

"I'm from the Zone, off Bloom," answered Cap.

"Oh, yeah?" Eddie said, paying for their food, before pulling out into traffic.

They dug into their shrimp baskets and curly seasoned fries, with a side of hush puppies.

"This shit famous," Hub Cab said with his mouth full.

Eddie nodded at the nucca, while thinking to himself. 'Nucca, you just don't know that's yo' last meal'…

Eddie pulled into the driveway of the spot on Dean off Outer Drive. Black was working on the crib, getting it ready for business, but they hadn't put any work in there yet.

"Come on," Eddie said, killing the engine.

Hub Cap followed Eddie through the side door of the crib. "Who else live here?" he asked, as they walked through the kitchen and out to the living room. "This all you playboy," Eddie said. Hub Cap was admiring all the latest stuff which plushed the spot.

"Shit, I can get used to this," Cap said, flopping down on the leather sectional sofa.

"Nah, we don't wanna get that dirty," Eddie said. "Sit in that one," he said pointing to a cloth sofa.

"I'll be right back. I gotta use the bathroom," Eddie said.

Hub Cap kicked his shoes off and grabbed the remote to the 54" floor model flat screen TV. He was grooving to Method Man's new video. He hadn't seen Eddie re-enter the room pointing the chrome Desert Eagle .44 square at his head. "You comfortable?" Eddie asked. Hub Cap looked up while saying "Yeah…." His mouth dropped. He looked like he'd seen a ghost. "Good," Eddie said, then squeezed the trigger. Boom! Boom! Boom! He splattered Hub Cap's brains all over the wall and sofa. 'I told you we weren't tryna' get that shit dirty," Eddie said, looking at his work….

Chapter Six

"I was wondering when you nuccas were gon' come see me," I said, as Nick, Black and Eddie entered the hospital room.

"You know we weren't goint to miss you coming home," Nick said giving me dap.

'Yeah, fool. We wouldn't miss it for the world," Eddie said, showing me some love.

"I'ma step down to the Gift Shop, Coach," Jackie said, excusing herself from the room.

"I know that ain't ole' girl from the Fox?" Nick said.

"Yeah, she was with me when I got hit."

"What's up with her?" asked Nick.

"She solid. Real good people. They say she saved my life. What's up, Black, man, you ain't gone show ya' man no love?" I asked.

Black was still standing by the door. He had tears in his eyes. "We should have been there for you, Coach man. I shoulda been there," Black said, sounding all emotional.

"I'm good, my nucca. Nucca ain't do nothin' but hit me a few times, but I'm still here. Nucca, I'ma warrior."

"I know," Black said crying. "But we, still shoulda' been there."

"What took ya'll so long to come see me? I was starting to think somebody had got at all of us."

"I couldn't come see you without handling B.I. first. Nuccas couldn't see you laying up in here with all this shit hooked up to you, and not have no blood on my hands," Black said.

"Who?" I asked clenching my jaw, as I knew where Black was headed.

"We got at Rome and them Buffalo nuccas coming outta the gas station on 7 Mile, and we flat lined that nucca Jason up at Romel's," Black said.

"That was ya'll? I seen that shit on the News."

"But that ain't all…" Black said walking over to the window.

"I was bout to say, cause I know them lil' nuccas wasn't tryna see us."

"You ain't gonna believe who's part of this?" Black said.

"That nucca, Rocko," he revealed. I didn't want to believe it. We weren't seeing eye to eye, true enough, but Rocko wouldn't want me dead. We came up from the sandbox together. He wouldn't violate like that. "Who told you that shit?" I asked.

"You remember the lil' nucca Hub Cap, right?"

"Thieving ass Hub Cap. The one who be breaking into everybody's crib?"

"Yeah, that's the one."

"What about him?"

"He says that he was the one taking shots at you coming out the clubs. He said Rocko put a ticket on yo' head cause we gettin' all the money in the Zone, and he wants you dead," Black said.

"And you believe the nucca?"

"The funny thing is, I do. I mean think about it, we ain't beefing with nobody else. Rocko has been actin' shady. And he's still mad about you circulating his statement he made on you through the Zone. I don't put it pass the nucca," Black said.

I hadn't seen it like that. Maybe because I never really thought about it. We were too busy getting money and stuntin' on nuccas, that I hadn't even noticed the silent enemy I had created in Rocko.

"Where the nucca Hub Cap at?" I asked.

"He's no longer with us," Eddie said, tapping the butt of his hammer.

The door opened, so we froze the game. It was the nurse. She had my chart in her hand. “Are you ready, Mr. Townsend?” she asked.

The doctor was discharging me. After three weeks of physical therapy. I was back on my feet. I still had a slight limp, though. There was a bullet lodged in my left hip. I had been hit eight times altogether. Four times in the chest, three in the legs and once in the face. The bullet that stuck me in the face stopped after hitting my back bottom tooth.

“Am I ready? Hell yeah,” I said.

“Good. They’re processing your discharge papers. You be sure and take care of yourself,” the nurse said leaving, as Jackie stepped in, pushing a wheelchair. “Who’s that for? I’m not gettin’ in that shit,” I said looking at the wheelchair.

“It’s just until we leave the hospital. It’s policy, Coach. Come on, let me help you out of bed,” Jackie said, letting the guard rails down on my bed. “Can ya’ll help me, I don’t want to drop him.”

Nick and Black helped Jackie lift me into the wheelchair, and she sat me up straight.

“Thank you for taking care of your man,” Nick said.

“Yeah, Coach. I think she’s a keeper,” Eddie said.

Jackie was blushing from ear to ear. I looked her in the eyes, and said, "I think so too, E."

*****

"Maybe you should consider moving, Coach. I mean at least until we can fix this," Nick said.

We were all sitting at the round table in the dining room. Jackie was in the kitchen putting a home-cooked meal together. And depending on how good her cooking was, she just might be a keeper.

"Maybe you should consider rolling me up a blunt, so I can get my lungs out the street," I said, tossing Nick a Swiser Sweet.

"I don't think it's a bad idea, Coach. Until we can find this nucca and murk him, you really shouldn't be laying yo' head here," Eddie said.

"Let me tell ya'll something, my daddy ain't raise no track star. Once you start runnin', you'll be runnin' all yo' life. I tell you what I am gonna do, though. I am going to smoke this nucca outta hiding. And I'm gon' murk that ass personally. Ya'll done put enough work in. This nucca is mine. It's personal," I said.

"I already knew you were gonna say no to moving, which is why I ain't bring it up. But at least, let us put some nuccas around you to watch the house," Black said.

"You mean like some bodyguards?" I asked.

"Yeah," answered Black.

"Ain't no nucca bouts to throw they self in front of a bullet for me."

"I would," Eddie said.

"Besides ya'll. We all we need. Us right here. Crew, fuck that side-show shit. It's easy. I'ma find this nucca and kill em'," I said, as Jackie entered the room carrying two large platters above her head.

"Damn, that shit smells good," Black's greedy ass said rubbing his stomach.

Jackie sat the fried chicken down on the table, then brought back all the sides; fried cabbage, sweet Jiffy corn bread, black eyed peas, and a pitcher of Cherry Kool-Aid.

"Enjoy!" Jackie said confidently, then kissed me on the cheek.

Yeah, she had earned her spot with that meal…

Chapter Seven

"Baby, where are you going? It's only 6:30 in the morning?" Jackie said rolling over and looking at the alarm clock.

I was fully dressed and was lacing up my Timbs. I stood up and kissed Jackie on the lips then brushed her long blonde hair to the side of her face. "I gotta handle some B.I., I shouldn't be long though," I said kissing Jackie again, before hitting the door.

"Be careful!" she yelled, as I slammed the door.

Jackie had spent the past few nights with me. Nah, who am I kidding, she had moved in. We just hadn't talked about it. As much as I appreciated her helping me bounce back, I also enjoyed her company. The streets were calling and I had a war to win…

I jumped in my white 500 and peeled off. I could see two nuccas parked in a Dodge Stratus two houses down through my rear-view mirror. They had been out there every day since my release from the hospital. Black thought he was slick, like I didn't know he hired them two rookies to watch my back. I played the rear-view until I reached Nevada, sure enough the Stratus was pulling away from the curb. I stomped on the gas opening up the Benzo's pipes. By the time the Stratus turned onto Nevada, I was twelve blocks down and turning down Lamont. I laughed to myself "Rookies..."

What I was about to do, I didn't need nobody tailing me. I popped in Biggie's Ready 2 Die CD, and turned it to my favorite song. I sat up gripping the wheel as the lyrics poured through the speakers, "Somebody's got to die. If I go you got's to go," I sang along to the chorus.

That's exactly how I felt. If Rocko wanted me dead, then he had to go first.

I pulled into Exotic Cars where I bought my Benz. I was looking to trade mine in for another one. Everybody in the city knew I was pushing the white Benzo, and it was too easy to spot, so I wanted to switch up. I saw a triple black 600 S-class Benz with limo tint parked near the front gate.

"Yeah, that's me right there," I said getting out the car.

"Hey, hi you doing, kid?" The old man asked me.

"Making it, how 'bout ya' self?" I asked shaking the owner's hand.

"Business as usual. So, I see you've got your eyes on that Mercedes over there. She's a beauty, isn't she?"

"Yeah..." I said, admiring the car.

"And judging from the bumps in your pockets, I suspect you're ready to buy her? Shall we take her for a ride?" The old man asked.

"Nah, that won't be necessary. I want to trade the white one in, and pay the difference on the black one," I said.

The old man was a professional crook. He had the paperwork done and I pulled off the lot in less than an hour. I punched it down 8 Mile trying to get my thoughts in order. 'How can I hit the nucca, and make my presence?' I thought. An idea popped in my head. I pulled over at White Castle's on Sherwood, and used the pay phone.

"What up, dough," Nick said, answering the phone.

"Where Black and Eddie at?" I asked.

"They right here. I'm over here beating their ass in Street Fighter 2," Nick said.

"Well, pause the game 'cause some real street shit 'bouts to go down. Ya'll nuccas meet me at Pixie and Dixie."

"What the fuck is Pixie and Dixie?"

"Just tell Black, he'll know what I'm talkin' about," I hung up the phone and jumped back in the whip.

"Who was that?" Eddie asked, as he took a pull on his L.

"Coach. He said to pause the game and meet him at Pixie and Dixie," Nick said, sounding confused about the location.

"Come on. I know where it is," Black said, grabbing his car keys off the front counter of the detail shop. They all piled in Black's Benz and headed west on Davidson.

Black pulled into the parking lot of Pixie and Dixie on Conant. It was an old preschool/church. Black, Rocko, and Coach use to go there back in the day. Black scanned the lot, but no sign of Coach.

"Where this nucca at?" Black said, while parked at the entrance of the lot.

Beep! Beep! I rolled the window down and flagged Black over. I knew he couldn't know it was me because I had changed cars. I got out the car and posted on the hood, as Nick, Eddie and Black all joined me.

"Damn..." Nick said, walking around my new 600 in full circle. "That's how you feel? A nucca tries to kill you and you cop a six. I gotta step my shit up," Nick said admiring the ride.

"That's not why I called ya'll here," I said.

"Yeah, I was wondering why you got us standing in the parking lot of ole' Pixie and Dixie. What's up, my nucca, you a'ight?" Black asked.

"Yeah, I'm good," I said, hitting rocks with the crew. "The reason I had ya'll meet me over here is because what we bouts to do, we don't need nobody saying they saw us together, which is why I traded in my white Benz. Tomorrow, all ya'll got to do the same. Go holla' at the old man, and jump in something new," I said.

"What you got planned?" Eddie asked rubbing his hands together, like let's get it on.

"We 'bouts to burn the Zone to the ground. Every house and spot that ain't ours got to go. I don't give a fuck who's runnin' that shit, its coming down. Like I said, we gon' smoke that nucca ass out. You cut off a nucca water, and he bound to surface. A lot of bodies are 'bouts to start dropping, so we gotta be on point. If we need to meet up, it'll always be far away from the Zone. We can't get caught slipping either. So keep yo' shit on you at all times. And Nick, for now, stay outta them damn clubs. I know how you like to stunt, but we're at war right now…"

"Finally, some excitement," Eddie said.

"Oh yeah, here," I said, I popped the trunk. I handed each of them brand new bullet proof vests. They were from King David's stash.

"Keep these shits on for the next 30 days. I want you to eat, sleep, and shit with these shits on. I don't know if I could stand something happening to one of ya'll right now, so be careful." I said. "We Crew."

"Crew!" we all said, hitting rocks…

"Look, I'ma call ya'll tonight with the rundown. Be ready," I said jumping into my Benz.

I had been gone all day, and I wanted to spend some time with Jackie before I kicked this war off. I was rocking up just thinking about that little tight pussy of hers. I stepped on the gas trying to hurry up and get home. I turned down Caldwell, and as I crossed Hillsdale, I could see the two nuccas in the Stratus parked in front of Rocko's crib. As I passed the car, I looked inside, and what I thought were two heads, was actually the head rests. I kept driving to the end of the block and turned down Stockton, then drove up the alley leading to the Pit-bull farm. I opened the privacy fence, and parked dead center of the farm. I didn't want anyone to know what car I was driving, so I figured it would be best I parked back there.

I jumped the fence leading into my backyard, and walked around to the kitchen's sliding door. All the lights in the crib were now off, but I had remembered them being on when I drove pass. Something just didn't feel right. I pulled my .45 from my pants, then quietly slid the door open. I crept through the kitchen ducked low in case someone took a shot at me it would go over my head. Stepping into the darkness of the living room, I heard a sharp wind coming my way. I side stepped and I heard a loud crashing sound of glass shattering against the wall. My legs came from under me, as I started firing my hammer. Boom! Boom! Boom!

I no longer felt the pressure of someone's death grip on my legs. The front door opened, providing the only light throughout the house. A shadow bolted through the frame of the door heading for the porch. I let off two quick shots, Boom! Boom! Both shots missing the intended target and blowing two gigantic holes through the door frame. I scrambled to my feet, and ran out of the front door in pursuit of ole' boy. The headlight of Dodge Stratus parked in front of Rocko's house came on, and the tires violently burned the ground as the car peeled off. Boom! Boom! Boom! I ran into the middle of the street firing into the passing car. I could see the man duck low and grab his shoulder as he passed me. Boom! Boom! Click. Click. I was out.

"Damn!" I yelled. That bitch nucca got away, I thought. I cursed the air, as I stood in the middle of the street, gun smoking. People started coming outside trying to be nosy.

I yelled, "What the fuck is ya'll nosy asses lookin' at?"

I walked back inside the crib and flicked the living room light on. There was a black bald headed nucca laying dead on the floor. He must have been the nucca wrestling with me, I thought. I closed the door and walked over to the nucca. I kicked him as hard as I could in the face to make sure he was dead. The nucca didn't budge. "Ah. Shit," I thought. Where the fuck is Jackie? I tore out running through the crib, calling her name. "Jackie!" I yelled… "Jackie!" I yelled, as I stepped into the bedroom.

There she was all tied up, sitting in a chair. I raced over to her and pulled the scarf out of her mouth, and quickly untied her.

"Coach," she said wrapping her arms around my neck. She was crying her eyes out.

"It's okay. It's okay," I told her. I hugged her and squeezed her, trying to calm her down.

"It's not okay, Coach," Jackie said, pushing me back. Someone is out to kill you, and all you can say is it's okay!" Jackie screamed.

"Baby, come here," I said, trying to wrap my arms around Jackie.

"No Coach, stop. I want you to take me home now. And if you had any sense, you'd leave too," Jackie said, as she started gathering her things.

"I'ma fix this Jackie, I swear," I said.

"Well, when you do, call me," Jackie said, storming out of the room.

I flopped down on the edge of the bed and put my face into my hands. Deep down, I knew Jackie was right, but I couldn't leave. I wasn't about to start running.

"Ahh…" Jackie screamed.

I jumped up and ran into the living room where Jackie was at. She was standing over ole' boy's dead body. "He can't hurt you anymore," I said, leading Jackie back into the kitchen.

"Look Jackie, I really appreciate all you've done for me these past few weeks, I do. But this is my life, it's who I am. You're right. Somebody is trying to kill me. And I'm not going to let em'."

"Coach, you should know by now that I'm down for you, otherwise I would have left you at the hospital. But this is just too much for me. It's one thing to be in the streets, but when you start bringing the streets to where you live, that's when it becomes a problem. Them two fools could have raped me, killed me, or whatever else…" Jackie said, getting emotional again. "I didn't know where you were. I thought that they were going to kill you when you got home," she said.

"Let me take you home. We can finish talking on the way," I said, opening the patio door. I pulled the Benz from the farm and had Jackie meet me in the alley. As we drove, I wrecked my brain as to where I had seen ole' boy, who was still laying in my living room. I couldn't place it, but I definitely knew the nucca from somewhere. I was so lost in my thoughts of war, I hadn't said a single word to Jackie the whole drive to her house.

"So, I guess this is it?" Jackie said, as we pulled in front of her mom's house.

"You think I would play you like that?" I asked.

"It wouldn't be the first time," Jackie said, cocking her head to the side to face me.

"That was different," I said, smiling. "But nah, seriously though," I grabbed Jackie's hand. "I could never forget about the woman who saved my life. Just as soon as this is over, we'll be together. I promise. And you know I don't make cheap promises."

Jackie smiled for a moment. "Well, you just promise me this. That this will be the last time leaving me."

"I promise," I said.

Jackie leaned over and kissed me. There was just something about the way that she touched me, that made me feel like I didn't want to be anywhere else in the world, except with her. That feeling was getting the best of me, but I had to fight it. I gently pushed Jackie back, then said," I gotta go."

"You be careful," she said.

She kissed me once more, and then got out of the car. I watched her to the door before pulling away from the curb. I had to shake that lovey dovey shit, I told myself. I turned on the radio, and my nucca Biggie filled the car. "Somebody's got to die. Let the gun shots blow…"

Chapter Eight

I stopped at the pay phone on Livernois to call Black and let him know what went down. He was at the detail shop still playing Super Nintendo with Nick and Eddie. "For real?" Black asked, as I briefly ran it all down.
"I'm on my way to the crib right now. Meet me there, but park in the alley behind the farm," I said hanging up the phone. I punched the Benz down 7 Mile running every light that tried to catch me. I felt like a real live mob figure pushing the six. I could see the reflection of that black beast in the windows of the assorted businesses on 7 Mile as I weaved in and out of lanes. I was definitely about to start carrying it like the mob. Mothafucka's was about to come up short like back when the Purple Gang ran the city back in the day. I had Biggie's song on repeat. It had become my anthem.

"Let the gun shots blow…" I could see the ass end of Black's Benz sitting in the farm as I pulled around it. He Nick and Eddie were waiting in the living room. "You know who this is?" Black asked me as I stepped into the room. He was standing over ole' boy.
"Nah, who is it?"

"That's Midget. Felicia's lil' brother," Black said.

"Get the fuck outta here," I said turning my head side ways to look at the nucca's face. "Sho' is…"

I hadn't seen Midget since I went up to Green Oaks for killing the two nuccas. I didn't recognize him at first because he had grown. Well, his face had matured. His body hadn't grown much, which is why he got the name Midget. He was a real life midget.

"What happened?" asked Black.

"I came through the back door and all the lights were out in the crib, so I pulled my hammer out. When I stepped into the living room, this' lil' bitch tried to tackle me, but I lit his ass up."

"So, what's these holes right here in the door?" Eddie asked, rubbing his hands across the door frame.

"When I dumped this faggot, another nucca ran out the door."

"You ain't get him?" asked Nick.

"Nah, the bitch nucca lucked out. I had em', but I ran out of bullets. For, real, I had thought you had them lames watching me," I said looking at Black.

"What you mean?" asked Black.

"They had been sitting outside parked in a Dodge Stratus for the past few days."

"Was it light blue?" asked Black.

"Yeah."

"That's that lil' nucca Scrap. That's his momma's car," Black said.

"Well, let's go pay lil' Scrap a visit," Eddie said.

We all piled into my six with Nick taking the wheel, and me riding shotgun. Black was in the back with Eddie blowing an L, and giving Nick directions. "Slow down," Black said, as we came to a slow creep down Anglin Street. "See, right there," Black said, pointing to the light blue Stratus parked in the driveway. I could see bullet holes in the passenger side door, and the window was shattered. We kept going and Nick turned into an old laundromat that sat on the corner.

"This what we gon' do," I said turning in my seat to face the Crew. Nick, you gonna knock on the door and ask for directions, or ask to use the phone. As soon as they let you in, up mag on they ass. Black and Eddie, ya'll cut through the alley and come around back in case the nucca tries to run again. I'ma play the bushes. I'm right behind you, Nick. Kill everybody in the house," I said, before I cocked my .45.

"I'm ready," Eddie said, blowing out a thick cloud of smoke.

We all hit rocks, then took our positions.

I cut out on foot heading down the block with my hoody pulled over my head. I slid into the bushes next door to Scrap's crib, and waited. A few minutes later, Nick bent the corner and pulled in front of the house. He got out and walked up to the front door, than rang the door bell. I heard the door open, and Nick went into his spill.

"Sure, I heard the voice of a woman say, then the screen door swung open.

"Bitch, you betta not scream," Nick warned, as he put the barrel of his .380 to the woman's stomach.

I was right behind him. Nick held ole' girl at bay, while I motioned through the house securing each room. I opened the side door for Black and Eddie, and put my finger to my mouth, like shhh….

"Ma, who is that at the door?" a man's voice called out. His footsteps grew louder, as he came down the stairs.

I stepped into the hallway and raised my gun pointed dead for the stairwell.

"Who is that, Ma?" Scrap asked when he reached the bottom step. He saw the pistol sticking out and tried to haul ass back upstairs.

Boom! Boom! I let off two shots up the stairs, neither hitting the lame. I started up the stairs after the nucca.

Boom! Boom! The nucca was busting back. He caught me twice in the chest causing me to fall backward down the stairs. Boom! Boom! Scrap let off two more shots. Black and Eddie raced to pick me up.

"You a'ight, my nucca?" Black asked, kneeling.

I tapped my bulletproof vest, then stood to my feet. "Now, let's go get the bitch," I said, taking the lead with Black on my heels.

We inched up the stairs and turned around the banister. The nucca Scrap was on his way out the window. He had one leg out and one leg still inside. I ran over to the window and grabbed the nucca. He was trying to break free and was reaching for his pistol.

"Let me help you with that," I said, standing back. Boom! Boom! Boom! I hit the nucca in his rib cage. He let go of the window pane and fell free to the ground. On his way down, Black stepped into the living room, I could see Eddie and Nick standing over Scrap's momma. Nick had his gun pointed dead at her head.

"What you want me to do with her?" Nick asked.

"Kill that bitch," I said walking out the front door. Boom! Boom!

"So, what's next, my nucca?" asked Eddie, as we drove down 7 Mile.

"I hate to do it, but Felecia's," I said. "Let me hit that," I said taking the blunt from Eddie. I knew I'd have to be high for this next one.

Chapter Nine

We stopped by Black's detail shop, so we could grab some bigger guns. If we were going to hit Felicia's crib, we were gonna need some fully automatic weapons, because on any given day there would be a house full of people at Felicia's. And that's exactly how I wanted it…

"Let us out at the alley," I said as we bent the corner. We were driving the Le Sabre.

"What you want me to do?" asked Nick.

"Circle the block in about five minutes, we should be ready by then."

"What? That's it. I want to put some work in too," Nick said.

"Nucca, you killed one mothafucka, and now you's a killa'," teased Eddie.

"Just chill, Nick. We need you behind the wheel. Come on, ya'll," I said climbing out the car with Black and Eddie in tow.

We crossed the street and hit the alley, which sat across from Felicia's house. We came up through the back yard of an abandon two family flat and kneeled down on the side of the house. "How we gonna make it inside the house? Look at all them nuccas," Black said.

"One thing about nuccas, though, when gun shots ring out, they do what?" Without waiting for an answer, I stood up and took full speed crossing the street. I started bustin'. Laaka! Laaka! Laaka!

Just as I suspected, nuccas took off running in all directions. My focus was on the house. I ran full speed up the frontporch steps and kicked the screen off the hinges. Laaka! Laaka! Laaka! I let off three shots stepping into the living room. I hit two chicks in the chest who were sitting on the sofa doing their nails. Laaka! Laaka! I hit Phil the mechanic in the back as he tried running out the front door. Boom! Boom! Boom! Three shots whistled past my head planting into the dry wall behind me. Laaka! Laaka! Laaka! I returned three shots in the direction where the shots were coming from. I could hear Black and Eddie outside putting in work. Laaka! Laaka! I let off two shots down the empty hallway as I inched toward the kitchen.

I could see a shadow leaning against the refrigerator. I put the barrel of my gun to the wall where I'd seen the shadow and let it ride Laakaaa.... I heard a body hit the floor, so I kept moving toward the back of the house. I stopped at the bathroom door and was about to open it, but something told me not to. Finally, Eddie and Black entered the house. They stood beside me and I put my hand to my mouth, like shhh… Eddie pushed me to the side and kicked the door open. Boom! Boom! Boom! Three shots licked off sending Eddie stumbling backward. Black's eyes bucked as he sprang into action. He hit the bathroom blazing. Laaka…. Laaka… When the smoke cleared, Felicia's lifeless body laid slumped over the tub. She was still gripping the butt of her pistol. Black and I looked at her for a moment, and then tended to Eddie.

"You straight, my nucca," I asked.

Eddie was holding his chest. "The bitch tried to stank me," laughed Eddie. "But bitch, I'm bulletproof," Eddie said looking at Felicia, and banging on his vest. We all bust out laughing.

"Let's get the fuck out of here," Eddie said.

Beep! Beep! Nick was outside hitting the horn. "Ya'll ready?" he asked as we walked out the house.

"Pop the trunk," I said.

"What? The police will be here in a minute," Nick said.

"And we'll air they asses out, too. Pop the fuckin' trunk," I said.

Black and I grabbed the two gas cans and went back inside the house. I wet upstairs, and Black doused the bottom floor with gas.

"You ready?" I asked Black. He was still hitting the sofa where the two bitches laid dead.

"Yeah, let's do it."

Eddie was standing at the door with a lighter in one hand and a newspaper in the other hand. As Black and I exited the house, Eddie lit the paper and tossed it inside the house. By the time we were in the car and pulling off, the whole house was ablazed…

"Where to now, my nucca?" asked Nick.

"You know the Zone 'bouts to be hot as E-mothafucka. Police 'bout to be all through this bitch," Black said from the back seat.

"I know. That's why we gon' switch cars and keep it moving. This is the best time to strike, while they busy dealing with one crime, we busy committing another one," I said.

"I like that shit," Eddie said firing up another blunt…

Eddie took it back to the old school with the flat head screwdriver. We had to switch cars and Eddie said he still had it. We pulled into the parking lot of Steve's Soul Food and parked while E-double did his thing. The nucca was so smooth, you'd think he had keys to the black Conversion van he was backing out.

"That nucca still got it," I laughed.

Nick followed Eddie around the corner and we all climbed into the van. Black had doused the Le Sabre with gas and set that bitch on fire.

"Let's ride," he said, climbing into the van with the gas cans.

We headed back east, taking the Davidson expressway coming up on Ryan. Within minutes, we were back in the Zone, and as we crept pass Buffalo, red and blue strobe lights filled the block.

"It looks like they got the whole 11th Precinct down there," Black said.

"That's good," I said.

This next play was against my better judgment, but Rocko was doing some of his best hiding, and the only way to smoke him out, I figured was to hit him where it really hurt, family. I knew Caldwell like the back of my hand. There wasn't a house on the block I hadn't been in, including the one Rocko had Amanda living in while he was in hiding. Black, Eddie and I were kneeled down in the backyard of Dump's old house. We were watching the house next door. Through the kitchen window, I could see Amanda standing at the sink doing dishes.

"Here's the deal. Don't kill no kids and leave Amanda for me. I need her alive to relay our message," I said standing.

We jumped the gate into Amanda's yard and crept up the backporch steps.

"On three," I said.

On count three, Black kicked the back door off the hinges.

"Ahh!" screamed Amanda, stepping back from the sink.

Black and Eddie disappeared through the crib. I was all on Amanda.

"Bitch, shut the fuck up before I kill yo' ass," I said.

"I don't have any money in here," Amanda said.

"Bitch, I didn't come for no money."

Amanda's eyes shifted around the kitchen, then she darted for the dish rack and tried to grab a butcher knife. I twisted her arm almost breaking it.

"Drop it, bitch," I said.

She let go, and the knife hit the floor.

I pimp slapped Amanda, sending her to the floor. She scooted into the corner while looking up at me. With fear in her eyes, she asked "What do you want?"

"For you to deliver a message," I said pulling my mask off.

"Coach?" Amanda asked in total disbelief.

"Bitch, shut up and listen. If you want to live, then you're going to do exactly what I say."

Black and Eddie walked into the kitchen with Rocko's two sons at gunpoint.

"Plese don't hurt them, Coach," Amanda pleaded with me.

The little boys ran over to Amanda, and she pulled them close to her.

"There ain't nobody else in the house, it's empty," Black informed.

"Listen, bitch, you are going to call Rocko right now. Wherever he's at, you're going to pick up the phone and get him on the line," I said.

"I'll do anything, just don't hurt us," Amanda cried.

"Here," I said, handing Amanda the kitchen phone. She dialed seven digits quickly, and I could hear the phone as it started ringing.

"Hello?" Rocko answered the phone.

"Rocko," Amanda cried into the phone.

"Baby, what's wrong? Why are you crying?"

"They're here, and they got me and the boys…"

"What? Who? Baby what's going on?" asked Rocko.

I snatched the phone from Amanda.

"Amanda, what's going on?" Rocko asked nervously.

"You gon' be a coward all yo' life, or you gon' face me like a man?" I said into the phone.

"Who is this?" Rocko demanded.

"It hasn't been that long, has it?" I asked.

"Coach?"

"Exactly. So, what you gonna do, we gonna meet up in the middle of Caldwell and do it like Warriors, or you gonna continue to hide like the bitch you are?"

"What the fuck is you talking 'bout, Coach? And why is you at my house?" Rocko asked.

"Nucca, don't insult my intelligence. I know you put some dust on my head. I know you shot me, bitch. But you know what, you bitch ass nucca, I'ma tell you something you don't know. I killed yo' daddy, Dump."

Rocko didn't say anything…

"Yeah, that's my work. So, we can stop tryna' kid each other. I'm tryna' see you, man to man," I said.

"Nucca, name a time and place," Rocko said.

My dick got hard hearing Rocko accept my challenge.

Meet me at Farwell Park in twenty minutes. I'll be standing in the middle of the field by myself. Bring yo' biggest gun, bitch."

"I'll be there," Click. Rocko hung up.

"What he say?" asked Black.

"He said he'd be there. Well, see," I said.

"What do you want us to do with them?" Eddie asked, looking at Amanda and her two boys,

"Ya'll get the fuck outta here," I told Amanda and her boys. "And Black, ya'll burn this bitch to the ground. I got a war to win," I said leaving out the back door.

I crossed the street and headed toward my crib. I opened the front door and ole' boy was still lying on my carpet dead. "You still here?" I asked laughing.

I went into the back and got some plastic and blankets. I rolled lil' Midget's ass up like a blunt in the plastic, then covered him up with the blanket. I tossed the nucca over my shoulder and carried him out back to the fire place on the back deck. I stuffed his little ass inside and doused the blanket with lighter fluid. I struck a match, then tossed it inside. The fire spread and after a few minutes, Midget's body was one big fire ball.

The smell of his burning flesh was awful. I had to hold my breath. I looked at my watch and it was time to meet Rocko at Farwell. I closed the grill to the fire place, and then went inside to grab my 50 cal. Desert Eagle.

Black and Eddie caught me as I was backing out in the Benz.

"You don't want us to come with you? You know that nucca ain't gon' play fair. He gon' have some nuccas with him," Black said.

"Yeah, you're right. And they gon' die with him, too. Look, I want ya'll to tail me in the van with Nick. Stay like five cars behind me. I'ma give the nucca a fair shake and meet him in the center of the field, but if shit don't look right, ya'll come blazing," I said.

"A'ight, my nucca. Be careful. We're gonna be right behind you," Eddie said.

"Yeah," Black added as we hit rocks.

I pulled off, Black along with Eddie climbed in the van with Nick.

"Where we going now?" asked Nick.

"Just tail Coach, but try to stay about five cars back," Black said.

"I'll be glad when all this shit is over, so we can go back to gettin' money. I need some pussy," Nick said.

"I feel you, my nucca," laughed Eddie. He was in the back of the van blowing yet another L.

Chapter Ten

I stood in the middle of Farwell Park in the pitch dark waiting on Rocko to emerge. Every sound, I flinched and turned in the direction of the noise, pointing my 50 cal. into thin air. It was only leaves turning over in the wind. I had been out there for two hours, and no sign of Rocko, or anyone else for that matter. I was furious… this coward mothafucka ain't coming, I told myself as I reluctantly put one foot in front of the other and headed back to my car.

"It's about damn time," Nick said, starting the van.

"What's up?" Nick said rolling down the driver's side window as I crossed the street.

"That bitch nucca ain't comin'. I shoulda' known he was gonna bitch up," I said, now standing at the van.

"I could have told you that. You know Rocko soft as pussy," Black said.

"Yeah, well let's get the fuck outta here. Meet me back at the crib," I said.

As I walked toward my Benz a pair of head lights popped on from across the street. They had them shits on bright damn near blinding me. I stopped in my tracks and put my hand to my face like it was a sun visor.

Another set of lights popped on to the rear of me. Then I heard car doors opening.

"Damn, they got us boxed in," I said.

"Coach! Look out! Yelled Nick.

Boom! Boom! Boom! Three shots ripped through the air lighting up the street. I ducked low behind the Benz, as more shots rang out from both directions. Boom! Boom! Laaka… Laaka… Boom! Boom!

My Benz was rocking like ten people were trying to tip it over. The windows were shattering on by one, then a bullet struck the back tire where I was crunched down at. I got's to get outta here, I thought. I clinched the butt of my 50 cal. tightly, then went for it. I came up blazing toward the head lights facing my car. Boom! Boom! I licked off two shots, buying myself enough time to make it behind a huge Oak tree. Boom! Boom! Boom! Three chunks of wood flew from the tree as I tried to stick my head from behind the tree.

I got low and scanned the block. There was six nucca's on each side of the block. We were out numbered without a doubt, but we weren't going out without a fight. Boom! Boom! Two more shots echoed through the night and rested in the tree. I back-stepped from the tree, dumping. Boom! Boom! Boom! I made it to the side of this house, a few yards away from the Benz. Boom! Boom! Click. Click. I was out. I slid another clip in and racked one into the chamber.

"We gotta get out this van if we gone make it outta here alive," Eddie said crunched over in the back seat. Nick and Black were doing the same thing. They were curled up into balls nearly touching the floor mats.

"Ya'll hear me?" Eddie yelled over the gun fire.

"Yeah, I hear you, my nucca. Come on, let's go get these bitches," Black said reaching for is AK-47 Russian model. The van was rocking as Rocko's team fired non-stop into the windows and doors.

"Nick, slide over here. And on three we up," Black said.

"Three," Black said hitting the passenger door gun blazing. He let his AK-47 ride out while Nick scrambled out the van. Laaka!

Eddie hit the back door with his AK-47 spittin' like a fire breathin' dragon. He flatlined three nucca's with his first ten shots. Laaka! Laaka! Nick was at Black's side squeezing off rounds from his Tec-9. He dropped this one nucca in the middle of the street, and caught another nucca five times in the back, as he ran for cover. The Crew was representing, but my focus was on Rocko.

"Where you at, bitch?" I said, still kneeling on the side of the house. I saw someone waving their hand, like come on. The Crew was serving them fools, and they were trying to retreat. I locked eyes on this one nucca sitting behind the wheel of one of the cars that had hit its lights. It was Rocko. He turned and locked eyes with me for a moment. Here it was, all his men were out here on the battlefield, and he was doing what he does best, hiding. The sight of the bitch nucca brought me to my feet. His eyes widened and I could see the rear lights flick as if he'd put the car in drive. I came out blazin. Boom! Boom! Boom! I planted three slugs into the tires, flattening them. Then I put another four shots into the engine block. Rocko tried to speed off, but crashed into my Benz.

I slid another clip in, and walked toward the car with my gun pointed at the driver's side door. Rocko looked as if he'd seen Satan himself, as I approached the car. He fiddled with the door handle, but couldn't get it open. I reached inside with one hand, and snatched Rocko out of the car. He slid to the ground, and with that death look in his eyes, he began begging for his bitch ass life.

"Come on, Coach. We're family man. Whatever Dump and King David had going on is between them. I don't care about that shit, my nucca."

"And neither do I," I said standing over Rocko.

"Then we can go back to how it used to be. To us being crew. Fuck all that money, cars, jewelry, and other bullshit. I'm sorry, Coach," Rocko pleaded, dropping a tear.

I lowered my gun halfway, then raised it back up to Rocko's head. I dropped a lone tear, then said, "I'm sorry, too. But it can never go back to the way it was, we ain't crew no more." Boom! I melted Rocko's grill, then stood over him and cooked his chest. Boom! Boom! Boom!

Black came running up behind me to see Rocko's dead body.

"Damn," he said.

That's all that could be said. Rocko was like family, but he had violated and that was the end result.

"Come on ya'll! Yelled Nick from the van. I took one last look at Rocko, then climbed into my Benz and pulled off. I rode the rims all the way home with the deflated tires from the gunshots. I had left a part of me back there, I thought, as I looked in the rear-view mirror…

Chapter Eleven

The war was over, Rocko was dead and gone. It was messed up how it had ended between us. I loved the nucca like a brother. But that's the game. And so far I had lost nearly everyone close to me, except Tina and Black. They were the only two left in my life who'd been there since day one. Now that the war was over, it was time to put all that behind me and get back to living my life. Me and the Crew had money to get, and nuccas to stunt on…

*****

"What did you do to her?" asked the old man at Exotic Cars, as we exited the dealership office. The Benz was mounted on the back of a flat bed. All its windows were busted, headlights shot out, tires flat, and so many bullet holes filled the car it looked like a target sheet from the gun range.

"I had a lil' accident?" I said.

"Where, in hell?" asked the old man.

"Don't worry about it," I said, mocking the man's accent. I put my arm around his shoulder, and then pointed at Black. "You see this bag my friend here is carrying? You're a pretty smart man, you know what's inside the bag. It's enough to cover the damages and to put me and my friends here in four new ones," I said, then nodded to Black to hand over the money. The old man clutched the bag and took on a brand new attitude. "You see, now who says money can't buy you happiness," I said.

We all bust out laughing.

"Which one you want, Black?" I asked waving my hand around at all the cars as if I owned the lot.

"Shit, we should switch up from the Benz and kill em' in something else," answered Black.

"Yeah, let's do something ain't nobody else in the city doing," Nick said, scanning the lot.

"Like what? What you think E-double?" I asked, Eddie. He was rolling up his morning blunt.

"Shit. Whatever ya'll want is cool with me," Eddie said, licking his Swiser, then splitting it down the middle with his thumb nail.

I looked around the lot and locked eyes with this triple black thang sitting on chrome. "What the fuck is that?" I asked no one in particular, as I started walking toward the car. The closer I got, the more I was falling in love. The Crew was on my heels. We all stopped and examined the car. "Oh, shit. This that new Maseretti," Nick said, pointing at the pitch fork symbol on the grill.

I opened the door and got in. The shit was plushed with Italian leather and wood grain everywhere. I liked it, cause it was luxury, but it still felt like a racing car. The old man appeared at the driver's side door.

"I see you've found your new toy."

"Yeah, but I need three more," I said, getting out.

"Not a problem. I will call the dealership and have them bring me three cars right away. Any specific colors?" asked the old man.

Black, Nick and not so much Eddie were giving the old man their colors like little kids inside of Toys R' Us.

"Nucca, we 'bouts to kill em,'" Nick said, excitedly.

"Well, ya'll deserve it after all that work we put in. And that's why we're Crew," I said.

"No doubt," E-double said giving me some dap.

"So, what we gone do now?" asked Black.

"Shit, we go back to getting this money. Life don't stop, cause one nucca got shot," I said.

"That's what I'm talking about, let's get this money," Nick said rubbing hand together.

"Speaking of money. Did you holla' at yo' dad, Nick?" I asked.

"Yeah. We're on for 2:00," Nick said, looking at his watch. So, we got about an hour before we gotta be there."

After a little while, a yellow freight turned up in the car lot with Black, Nick and Eddie's Maseretti's on its racks. We all raced over to the freight excited, and watched as the driver unloaded each toy one by one. Black's was navy blue, Eddie's was hunter green, Nick had the fire engine red box, and I was in the triple boy. All our shits was on chrome.

"Look, me and Nick gone get up with ya'll in a minute. Meet us at my crib in 'bout an hour," I said hitting rocks with Black and Eddie. "Let's see how these shits ride," I said, jumping behind the wheel.

I let the tires spin out, and then smashed out. Nick was right beside me as we flossed down Kelly Road, then turned onto 7 Mile. We were flying, switching lanes, and hitting our exotic horns at hoodrats. We must've turned every head on 7 Mile. We took the mile up to Outer Drive and turned left by the cemetery and rode until the street changed to Conner's. We pulled into the parking structure for private flights and parked.

"Do you see him?" I asked Nick through the window.

"Nah, let me go see if he landed yet," Nick said, as he headed for the small terminal of the City Airport.

A few moments later, Nick stuck his head out of the terminal door and waved me over. I started the car and followed Nick onto the tarmac where Torch was waiting outside the plane. Like clockwork, we went to unload the boxes from the plane and put them in the trunk of my car. There was no hey, how you doing?- type of shit. It was all business. Get this dope, pay me, and let's get the hell out of here. That was Torch's attitude. As soon as the last box hit the trunk, I handed Torch an army size duffle bag with the weight of a ten year old boy in it. He threw the bag inside the plane, climbed in, and shut the door. I jumped behind the wheel and followed Nick back out into the parking structure, where he got in his car and tailed me. This time, though, we were doing the speed limit and wearing our seat belts. I had 300 bricks in the trunk. One wrong move and it was life under the jail. I was on egg shells the entire ten-minute drive back home.

I let out a deep sigh of relief as we turned off 7 Mile onto Caldwell. I wiped my forehead of the little beads of sweat, and unfastened my seat belt. I had made it again… Black and Eddie were already at the crib. Their Maserettis sat out front, looking like new money. I honked the horn and pulled into the driveway. Eddie and Black came out and helped me and Nick carry the boxes inside the house. "A'ight, ya'll know what time it is, out," I said, waving my hand for everybody to leave the kitchen.

"You putting us out?" asked Eddie.

"Ya'll know I don't like nobody watching me while I cook up. That shit is bad luck," I said. It wasn't bad luck. Truth is, I wasn't trying to part with the jewels Tina had given me. We were all Crew, but there were some things you just keep to yourself, especially if it's vital to your means of survival.

"You ain't got to tell me twice. I'ma be in the living room beating these nuccas heads in on that new Street Fighter," Nick said, racing out the kitchen.

Black and Eddie were on his heels.

"I got first," Black yelled.

I went into the pantry and pulled out all my tools. I had bought a mixing bowl from the Salvation Army; it was one of them kind you'd see in a bakery. It was a little old, but it got the job done. I sat the mixer on the counter, then grabbed all my cuts from the cabinets' baking soda, Miami Ice, and Benzocaine. I busted one of the brown boxes open with a butcher knife, and pulled 10 keys out, placing them on the counter next to the mixer. Using the knife, I split each key down the middle and dumped it inside the mixer.

I reached under the sink and got my whale sized scale and weighed out 2,500 grams of Benzocaine and Miami Ice, I tossed it into the mixer, then eyed the amount of baking soda I was gonna need to bring all this back. I started the mixer on low for a few minutes, then medium for five minutes. I was nodding to C-Bo's new shit. "Standing in the kitchen, palms itchin' 'bouts to whip up the quarter chicken," I sung the lyrics.

While the work was being mixed, I ran some water into a large cooking pot, and grabbed four Pyrex's from the cupboards. I weighed out nine ounces and put them into the Pyrex's, nine ounces in each one. I put the whip game down and turned the mix into butter yellow crack. I did this 15 times, until the mixing bowl was empty. I had turned those 10 bricks into 15 hard... That would last Black and Eddie three days tops, and then it was back in the kitchen. I was exhausted after whipping all the work, but I had to keep pushing. I dumped 10 more keys into the mixer on medium, while I went out to the pool house to grab my compressor.

I sat the compressor on the kitchen table, then started weighing out 500 grams and placing it inside the compressor. It was nothing but a metal box plate with a hammering pad on the center of the plate, which I placed on top of the mix, then used a slug hammer to compress the work back into a kilo. I was dripping with sweat from slamming the hammer down on the plate so many times. Once the plate moved passed a certain mark on the compressor, I knew that the mix had been turned into a kilo.

I slid each brick out of the box, and rewrapped them as if they had never been touched. The work was so good that I didn't have to worry about it not coming back when a nucca tried to cook it. As long as he didn't try to put the whip game on it, he was good. I didn't have to worry about it though, because only the old heads in the city had that game, and they were going to their grave with it.

"You in here making all this damn noise," Nick said, stepping into the kitchen.

I was wrapping up the last brick.

"You in this bitch like a mad scientist. Look at all this shit," Nick said, taking in all the paraphernalia around the kitchen. "You 'bout done?"

"Yeah, I was just finishing up. What time is it?" I asked, wrapping duck tape around the brick.

"It's huh, 7:30," Nick said, looking at his Roly.

"Damn, I been in here all day," I said, as Black and Eddie walked into the kitchen.

"Them eight right there is for you Black, and them seven is for you E. Let's get this money back going," I said, nodding to the 15 hard bricks sitting on the table.

"That's what I'm talking about, baby," E-double said, rubbing his hands together, then gathered up his work.

"I know the custo's probably way across town, we been shut down so long," Black said.

"But one thing about good product, it speaks for itself. They gonna be beating the doors down when they find out we back on," I said, stuffing the other 15 soft keys into a plastic grocery bag.

"What you 'bout to do with those?" asked Nick.

"It's called expansion," I said throwing the bag over my shoulder. "Come on, and ride with me, while these two nuccas go do their thang," I said, talking to Nick.

We all hit rocks and I shut down shop, putting all my tool away. Nick and I jumped in his Maseretti with the 15 bricks in the trunk. We headed west on 7 Mile. Before the war with Rocko kicked off, I had made a few contacts with some up-and-coming playas in the game. They had seen how hard the Crew was flooding and made some inquiries about some work. After doing my homework on the nuccas, I thought it would be a good look to fuck with them, cause they were in areas throughout the city I wasn't touching. I'd have to go to war with them nuccas before they just let me take over their hood, so I settled for the next best thing. I figured if I started supplying them nuccas with the work at a good price, then it would be just like I had opened my own spot in that area. I just had to spread the love, that's all.

We pulled up on Joy Road off the Southfield expressway and turned down Ashton. We were going to holler at this young nucca, Spoon. He was getting a few dollars over there with his crew. They called themselves the Joy Boys. We pulled in front of Spoon's crib and I got out the car and walked up to the front door, which was wide open.

"Nucca, bet I straight make it for a stack," I heard somebody say.

"Nucca, drop all that shit," another man dared.

I heard dice shaking, then they rolled against the wall. "Seven! Hah!" yelled the second man. "Two craps and a miss out. Get yo' crab ass back on the block. In here tryna' crawl up a nucca's leg. Yo' money too short," the man taunted.

Just as I was about to knock on the door, a man came brushing past me. By the shit face he was wearing, I took it, he was the one who had just lost.

"And when you get some mo' money, nucca. You know where I'm at," Spoon said taunting the man, as he stepped to the door. "Oh, shit. What's up Coach, man? What's good?" asked Spoon.

"Ain't shit, man. I told you when I got straight I was gonna holla," I said.

"Shit, I'm glad you caught me. I was just 'bout to re-up. For real, I thought you forgot about me."

"Nah, just had to tie a few loose ends, that's all. But uh, what you looking to get?"

"Shit, nothin' less than a brick?"

"And how much you paying?"

"Twenty-two. Sometimes twenty-three."

"Hard or soft?" I asked.

"What you mean?" asked Spoon.

I could tell that he wasn't up on game, and I damn sure wasn't about to wake em' up.

"Nah, I'm saying when you buy your work it's already cooked?" I asked.

"Yeah, 36 ounces."

I was screaming for joy on the inside. The nucca was getting juiced. $22,000 for a brick that was already cooked. Out of them 36 ounces, only about 26 ounces was real coke. The rest was blown up.

"Well, look. I got a sweet deal for you. I'ma give you 36 ounces in powder for $18,000. And I'ma even front you a brick for the same price. Whatever you cop, that's what I'ma front you," I said. I could see Spoon's eyes light up with dollar signs. Nobody in the city was letting em' go that cheap.

"The work, it ain't no garbage, is it?" Spoon asked, snapping out of his day dream.

"Nucca, I'd rather you slap my momma, than to insult me with a silly ass question like that. Hold on," I said, walking back to the car. I tapped the trunk and Nick opened it. I grabbed two keys out the bag and stuffed them into the sleeves of my coat, then closed the trunk. I walked back up to the porch and asked Spoon "You got a Pyrex?"

"A what? Spoon asked.

"Never mind," I said, shaking my head, as I walked into the house and into the kitchen. I scanned the kitchen in search of something to cook the work up in. I stopped on an empty Mayo glass jar sitting on the counter. It was filled with old rusty screws. I poured all the screws out in the sink, then searched the cabinets for a large enough pot. I filled the pot with enough water to cook up with and sat it on a burning eye of the stove. I opened the refrigerator and pulled a half empty Arm & Hammer baking soda off the door rack. I bust down one of the keys, and eyed about an ounce worth of coke, pouring it inside the Mayo jar. I poured about 7 grams of baking soda inside the jar, then ran some water over the mixture. The nucca Spoon was all over my shoulder as I carried the jar from the sink to the stove.

"Listen, I'ma give you this lil' bit of game cause I'm tryna' fuck with you. Plus, I don't have time to keep cookin' up for you. I'ma show you this one time, so pay attention," I said putting the jar inside the simmering pot. The game I was teaching Spoon was basic shit. I wasn't giving him the whip game that nucca had paid hun'd of thousands to learn. The lil' shit I was putting him on to was elementary. But you'd be surprised as to how many nuccas who called themselves hustla's didn't even know how to cook crack.

I pulled the jar from the boiling water and quickly carried it over to the sink and ran some cold water. I twirled the jar in a circular motion. "You see how it's turning into a gel," I said, holding the jar where Spoon could see. "Now watch this," I said, sticking the jar under the cold water, but only at its rim. I didn't want to chance cracking the jar, so I let it cool before shocking the work. I let some cold water seep into the jar and the gel turned into a solid rock, making clinking sounds as I continued to swirl the jar. I dumped the work onto a paper towel so it could air dry. "Voila!" I said, stepping back. "Now, have one of these fiends test that shit, and watch em' beat ya' door down," I said.

"Nah, I believe you. I can look at this shit and can tell this that butta. Hold on, I'll be right back," Spoon said, stepping out of the kitchen. He came back carrying an adidas shoe box. He handed it to me, and said "That's eighteen stacks."

"I'ma take ya' word for it, and run it through my money counter later on," I said looking inside the box at all the small bills. "Here. You owe me eighteen stacks for the other one," I said nodding to the two bricks on the table.

"A'ight. Good-lookin', Coach. Man, I'ma flip this and get right back on with you. That's my word," Spoon said, escorting me to the door.

We hit rocks and I jumped in the car with Nick.

"What took you so long?" asked Nick, starting the car.

"I told you, expanding. See the plan is to eventually have all these young nuccas who are up-and-coming, start shopping with us. We buy the work, and sell it whole. Fuck all that spot shit. That's slow money. Ain't no reason we shouldn't be doing a thousand bricks a month. Nucca, we 'bout to take our show on the road, too."

"What you mean?"

"Ohio, Indiana, Wisconsin, Nebraska. The whole mid-west basically. We gettin' our work so cheap, that we can expand into all these other States with no problem. We just gotta start hittin' all these events and mingle with nuccas from all over that's getting money."

"You mean like the All-Star Game and Super Bowl."

"Exactly... Now you feel me. Fuck just being local celebrities. Nucca, we're going for International. But first, we gotta lock Detroit down," I said.

"I see yo' vision, my nucca. Dr. King, ain't the only one who had a dream," Nick said.

We both bust out laughing.

"But nah, where we going now?" asked Nick.

"We gotta few more stops, then we can hit the bar and look for some titties," I said.

"Some titties... Titties are always good," Nick laughed, as we hit the John C Lodge.

I wanted to go drop some work on this little nucca Lex on the North End. His name was ringing in the streets and I really liked the nucca. He just came off as an official dude.

After we stopped and blessed Lex, we shot to Southwest to holla' at this Spanish kid, Jose. He was on some Latin King gang shit, some shit that nuccas in Detroit don't condone. But he wasn't causing me no harm, and Jose had Southwest Detroit in a head lock. I needed some of that money. The lil' mothafucka had some game about himself, too. He knew that the bricks had been bust down and put back together. He couldn't say he knew how to do it, but he knew what to look for. All in all though, the work was still A-1, so he shopped with me. Instead of $18,000 per brick, I let him get it for $16,000 plus the front. He ended up buying the last four, so I fronted him four.

In a day's work, I managed to secure three parts of the city. I was content with that because there were only four parts to Detroit. Spoon had the Westside; Lex was on the North End; Jose was in Southwest, and We had the Eastside. True, other nuccas were gonna eat, but as long as the Crew was getting the lion share, it was all good.

"Titties!" Nick yelled, as we hit the door to the Brass Key.

Butt naked chicks were everywhere.

"Ya'll miss daddy?" Nick asked opening his arms to hug two strippers who greeted us at the door, well, Nick, anyway.

I take it from the way the chicks were riding his dick, that he was a regular trick master in there.

"White boy Nick, where have you been, baby?" One of the young ladies asked, leaning in Nick's arms.

"This beast beside me has had me in hell. But I am now back in heaven. V.I.P. shall we?" Nick said, then escorted the two women to a booth.

I parlayed at the bar and watched the door for potential clientele. The way nuccas were throwing money around in the Brass, they had to be in the game. I was in there trying to network and build up contact…

Chapter Twelve

"May I help you, sir?" The receptionist at the Fox Theatre asked, as I approached the counter.

"Yes, I'm looking for a Miss Jackie…" I hadn't even had enough decency to get Jackie's last name.

"Help me out here, she's about 5'4", white girl, long blonde hair, and a big ole' butt," I said, describing Jackie.

"I hope that's not how my boyfriend describes me. But I think I may know who you're talking about," the receptionist said.

She was an old beat up body black chick with an ashy little afro perched on top of her head. She got on the intercom and paged Jackie. "Jackie Lappin, you have a visitor in the front lobby," she said speaking into the phone. "We'll see if that's her in just a minute," she said, then went back to doing her work.

I was suited and booted. I went down to Broadway's and bought a new blazer, then went over to City Slicker's to grab a pair of Ostrich cream color boots. It had been almost a month since I last saw Jackie, and I knew she thought I had forgotten about her, once again. For the past month, all I'd been doing is networking and expanding. The

Crew was copping 500 bricks every two weeks now, and them shit were sold before they touched the city.

I was staring out the window facing Woodward Avenue. I had been day dreaming. The receptionist pointed to me as Jackie entered the front lobby.

"Coach?" Jackie said, walking toward me.

"You say that like you're surprised to see me?" I said, turning around.

"Well, it has been what a month?" asked Jackie. She hadn't embraced me like I thought she would. She was standing back with her arms folded.

"Well, like I told you, I don't break promises," I said, trying to pull Jackie to me, but she pushed me away. "What's wrong?" I asked.

"You think that you can just put us on hold for a month, and then show up here and I'm supposed to be all over you?" Jackie said, with an attitude.

"Jackie, you know what I was dealing with. But that's all over and done with. I didn't want to keep going and coming. I made you two promises, remember? I promised that would be the last time I left you. Let me keep that promise," I said pulling Jackie to me. I looked deep into her eyes and continued my spill, "Baby, I'm here to stay. Can you forgive me?" I asked. I didn't wait for an answer I leaned in and took the answer I wanted. I passionately kissed Jackie for every bit of two minutes, then pulled her up for air.

"Grab ya' coat and purse," I said.

"Coach, I can't leave. I'm at work."

"Grab ya' stuff, and let them know you won't be coming back. My woman don't never had to work."

Jackie was grinning from ear to ear.

"Go on, I got a surprise for you," I said.

Jackie raced to the back.

"Depending on the beginning and ending of ya'll story, ya' might be able to make a good movie out of it. Cause that was one hellava scene right there," the old receptionist said, laughing.

Jackie came running out the back with her purse and coat.

"You ready?" I asked.

"Yeah," answered Jackie, taking my hand.

"That's right girl, run outta this mothafucka, and don't look back. God is good. Hallelujah…" The receptionist said, as Jackie and I hit the door.

I opened the passenger door for Jackie. My new Maseretti was parked at the curb.

"What happened to your other car?" asked Jackie as we pulled away from the curb.

"It's a surprise. A big surprise!" I said turning onto the Chrysler freeway. I turned the radio to 94.5, Oldies but Goodies were rocking. Luther Vandross's 'If this world were mine' was on. Jackie came to life. She sat up in her seat and turned the music up. "You know this is our song, right?" she asked, grooving to the song. "You probably don't even remember, do you?" she turned and asked.

"Of course, I remember. We danced to this song on New Year's Eve," I said.

Jackie reached over and kissed me on the cheek. We held hands and enjoyed each other's company, while riding through the plush streets of Troy, Michigan. Jackie oohed and ah'd at the mansions as we cruised down Liberty Ave.

"What would you do if you owned a house like that?" I asked, pointing to an estate two houses in front of us.

"I would never come outta the house. I'd be cooking, cleaning, and decorating," Jackie said, as I pulled into the estate's long stone parking area.

"You know who lives here?"

"Yeah, I've known ole' boy all my life," I said, parking near the front entrance. "Come on, I'll introduce you to him," I said getting out the car. Jackie followed me up the stairs, and stood at my side as I used the gold lion's head to knock on the thick double wooden doors.

"Maybe they're not home," Jackie said.

"Nah, he's expecting us," I said, then turned the door knob. "Ah, look, it's open."

Jackie and I stepped into the house, stopping at the entrance, and looked around at the empty living room.

"You sure someone lives here, Coach?" Jackie asked.

"Yeah, we do," I said, walking over to Jackie. I handed her the house keys, then gave her a kiss. "You might want to look at those keys. There's a key on there that belongs to your new Jaguar parked in the garage."

Jackie was speechless.

"It's okay, you can thank me later," I said walking over to the closet. I pulled out some home design magazine, and gave them to Jackie. "Now you can sit at home all day and design away. Just circle whatever you want, and I'll have it delivered."

"Coach, I don't know what to say."

"Say yes," I said, taking Jackie into my arms.

"Yes," she said, dropping a lone tear.

"Ah, baby. Why are you crying? We 'pose to be happy."

"I am. That's why I'm crying."

I wiped the tears from Jackie's face, then scooped her into my arms. I carried her up the spiral stairs to the master bedroom, and placed her on the bed. Jackie knew the drill.

She was out of her clothes and sprawled out across the king size bed in a sexy pose in seconds. My dick was standing at attention. I stood at the foot of the bed, stroking my dick back and forth in an upward and downward motion, while looking Jackie in the eyes. She was driving me crazy, she was sitting up with her back against the headboard and her legs bust wide open. She had one finger in her mouth, and playing with her pussy with the other hand.

She took the finger she had been playing with her pussy and gave me the 'come here finger.' I climbed in the bed and scooted to the top where Jackie now lay on her back with her neck arched up on two pillows. I mounted Jackie's face, sticking the head of my dick inside her pretty pink full lips. I began pumping Jackie's face as if it were her pussy, while looking down at my dick as it slid in and out of her mouth. Jackie was holding me by the waist, guiding me in and out of her lips. She was looking up into my eyes with that slutty look she'd give me whenever she was really trying to get me off.

I felt myself about to nut, so I pulled out, and began returning the favor. I rolled onto my back and pulled Jackie on top of me, helping her mount my face. She perched over on top of me as if she were riding a dick. She gripped the back of the headboard with both hands and started grinding my face like she was fucking me. I sucked on Jackie's clit until I felt her body start to jerk, and slowed down on her thrust.

My dick was so hard, and I was so geeked up, I couldn't take it any longer. I rolled Jackie off me into the doggy-style position, and slid the head of my dick inside the warm crack of Jackie's ass, then let it slide down the crack slowly and then into her pussy. "Ahh-shit," I sighed as I entered paradise. I stuffed my entire dick into Jackie's pussy and just let it rest there for a moment. "Shhhhit" I sighed, as I began to slow-stroking Jackie's soft ass, each stroke sending a ripple of waves through both ass cheeks. "Fuck me," Jackie pleaded.

I sped up my strokes keeping them long and deep, touching Jackie's G-spot with every thrust. The sight of her heart shaped ass slapping against my stomach was unbearable. I closed my eyes to try and block out the thought of busting. I reached around Jackie's waist and started playing with her clit, while hitting her from the back. I knew just how to get her off; I had done it several times in the past. I kept my pace and watched Jackie's face waiting for her to explode. She dug her nails into the sheets and moaned. "Corey, fuck… me…Ahh…"

I couldn't take Jackie moaning like that, she sounded so seductive. I leaned down over her and stuck my tongue in her mouth, while still digging her back out.

"Ahh" I sighed, while kissing Jackie's lips. I fell all the way inside her pussy and kept pumping, as I shot nut all up in her. We lay there sprawled out across the bed, all out of breath. I rolled onto my back and looked up at the ceiling, while Jackie lay across my chest, making small circles in my chest hair with her index finger. I looked her in the eyes and told her, "This is how it's 'pose to be."

For a long time in my life, I was finally happy. I hadn't felt like that since King David was alive. "I love you, Coach."

"I love you too."

Chapter Thirteen

I hadn't planned on selling the house on Caldwell. I wasn't parting with that crib for all the money in the world. I just felt if Jackie and I were going to be together, then she should feel comfortable in her own house. And that would be impossible for her to do that after those two lames tied her up in that house. Caldwell would be in the family forever, but for now, the Crew was using it as headquarters. Between the detail shop and Caldwell, that's where the Crew pretty much hung out. It had been a while since we all got together and stunted, so I bought us court side tickets to the Final Four in Cleveland, Ohio.

I wanted to get out and do some networking. Black, E-double, Nick and I drove our Maseretti's to Cleveland. We had to be the flyest nuccas on deck, hopping out them $120,000 machines. Chicks from all over were there, not to watch the game, but to trick off with all the ballers from across the map. Nick wanted to bring some broads from the city, some ole' stripper chicks, but I told him why would we bring some chicks that we could fuck any day of the week, when the baddest chicks in America were gonna be there waiting on us, and down to do whatever?

They had not disappointed us. We checked into the Marriott downtown. As soon as we hit the door, chicken heads and model chicks filled the hotel lobby. They were down there exchanging information and hooking up right there on the spot. This one pimp lookin' nucca had a stable full of exotic women you'd only see in magazines. He saw how the Crew hit the door decked out in diamonds and gold, with waist length chinchilla's on our backs. The nucca knew money when he saw it. He pulled up on Black while we were at the counter, and slid Black his card with his room number on it.

"Any one of these hoes," the pimp nucca said, looking in the direction of his stable.

Black showed us the card, and it said $500 for two chicks, per hour. Nick's freaky ass walked over to where the pimp was standing and struck a deal with ole' boy. The next thing I know, Nick waves us over toward the elevator. He was trick master for show. Nick bought all ten of them broads for the night. He paid the pimp in cash while we rode up on the elevator. We got off on the top floor and entered our presidential suite, with the women in tow. The pimp nucca rode back down on the elevator.

"Ya'll four comin' with me?" Nick said handcuffing the baddest four chicks, then headed for the bedroom.

I was straight for real. I was still good from that good nut off Jackie's ass, but a little head ain't never hurt nobody. I grabbed this petite lil' yellow bone by the hand and pulled her to the sofa with me. She had these thick full lips, she looked like she could suck the shit out of a dick.

"Where ya'll from?" ole' girl asked.

"Gator Capital," I said.

"Florida?"

"Nah, baby. Detroit," I said leaning back.

"Ertha, you hear that. They from Detroit city," ole' girl said, sounding country as E-mothafucka.

My antennas went up. "And where ya'll from?" I asked.

"Lexington, Kentucky," she answered.

"Oh, yeah. How is it out there as far as hustlin'? Is it a lot of money out there?"

"You talkin' about what, drugs?"

"Yeah. Is there a lot of crack heads in Lexington?"

"Hell yeah, white and black."

"And what's ya' name?"

"Shawanna."

"Aight. They call me Coach. I'ma have to pay you a visit down there soon. You don't mind showing me around, do you?'

"I'll do that for you. But what we gon' do right now?" Shawanna asked, scooting close me.

"Ain't no shame in my game, you ain't shamed, are you?" I asked pulling my dick out my pants.

"We all hoes in here," she said, then took my dick from me and slapped it in her mouth.

I was right. I knew a head hunter when I saw one. She was skulling the shit out of me. She had that good head you only see on porno tapes. Holding my dick with one hand at the base of it, with her head laid in my lap, she twirled her head in small circles concentrating on just the head of my dick. She used the saliva as lubrication to jack me off, while still circling my cap. The head was so good, my eyes started watering. I leaned back and exploded. Shawanna didn't miss a beat, she jacked and squeezed every ounce of nut out of me.

"Ah..." I reached down and grabbed her head, pulling her face up and down on my limp dick.

"You want some pussy?" Shawanna asked, sitting up. She was still jacking my limp dick, which was slowly rising. She was looking into my eyes, giving me that fuck me, this pussy is soaked and wet look. My dick rocked up in Shawanna's hand. "Or do you want some more head, baby?" she asked, flicking her tongue ring out her mouth.

Shit, if the pussy was as good as the head, then I was tryna' beat them guts up. I dug into my pants pocket and pulled out an ultra sensitive latex condom. I was about to put it on, but Shawanna took it from me and put it in her mouth. She wasn't biting it or nothin', she just had it on her lips. She leaned over and all in one motion using nothing but her mouth; she rolled the condom down on my dick, then sucked it a few times before sitting up. I ain't gonna lie, the lil' bitch was turning me on the way she was handling a nucca. She slid out of that lil' shit she had on, then pulled me off the sofa walking me over to an empty pool table in the middle of the floor.

"We gonna see who's ashamed," Shawanna said climbing onto the pool table.

Shit, I damn sure wasn't shame. I was game for whatever this lil' bitch had going…

She laid me on my back, dick sticking up to the ceiling. She squatted down over me in a cowgirl position, and held my dick in her hand as she slowly inserted the head. To my surprise, the pussy was still tight. She inched my dick inside her until all 9 inches were packed in. She reached one hand behind her, gripping my chest, and gripped my leg as support. That lil' bitch went to working that pussy on me like she was back home riding a bull. With each thrust, her camel toe scrubbed my pelvis.

"Ahh… shhit… ahh… shit," I groaned and moaned. I ain't never had no chik fuck me like that. Shawanna was looking up at the ceiling with this sexy ass fuck face, mouth half open and softly moaning. I started shooting nut everywhere. I laid back on the table out of breath, as Shawanna climbed off me.

"Yeah, we definitely gotta stay in touch," I told her.

"That's what they all say," she said smiling. But we'll see what's up."

I looked around the suite, there was nobody stuntin' the little shit we were doing. Black had two bitches on the balcony. One was eating the other one's pussy, while Black was creaming her from the back. My nucca E-double big cock strong ass, had this thick Oriental lookin' chick in the buck. He had her legs pinned behind her head holding them with one hand and fucking ole' girl in her ass. He was long stroking that shit like it was some pussy. And Nick freaky zeaky ass, ain't no telling what he had them four hoes back there doing.

We parlayed with them hoes for the night, then hit the Final Four the next day. It was supposed to be a two day event, but we missed the final game, because one of Black's workers said that homicide had been looking for us.

"What he mean they're lookin' for us?" Nick said.

We were on the elevator on our way down to the lobby so we could check out. Black had called to check on this operation when he got the news.

"Calm down. Don't nobody know who you are Nick. They just know your name is White boy Nick. They lookin' for me and Coach," Black said.

"For what?" I asked.

"I told Malcolm not to get specific, cause we were on the phone. But who knows?" answered Black.

"Somebody had to see us," Eddie said.

"Nah, Oh, shit…" I thought about Amanda.

Black shook his head at me. He knew me like a book, and knew exactly what I was thinking about.

"You can't keep saving that bitch, Coach," Black said, as the elevator door opened.

"What's he talking about?" asked Nick, but no one answered.

The entire drive back, all I could think about was how I had jeopardized the Crew and all that we grind for. And on the strength of what, a bitch? Amanda, the same bitch who left me for dead when I caught them two bodies. The same bitch who ran off with $70,000 and didn't send me a dime for five years. The same bitch who had not one, but two babies with my best friend.

What the fuck am I tripping on? I looked in the mirror and asked myself. There ain't but one thing to do…

Chapter Fourteen

I told the Crew to stay under the radar until we found out exactly what was what. That meant no clubbin', no stuntin' and no Zone. We'd have to move at night when we knew the 9-5 detectives were off duty, and even then, we had to be careful. I told them nuccas to park their whips, too, and jump in something else. We split up downtown at Belle Isle where King David had been laid to rest.

"Call me if anything jumps off, or if ya'll hear something," I said, still standing at the river bank.

Black, Nick and Eddie all jumped in their cars nervously. I turned and looked out into the water. "Ahh…" I let out a deep sigh. "Hey Pops, how you doing, man? I know it's been a long time since I've come to see 'bout you. I still haven't quite yet accepted the fact that you're gone. I finally see what you mean by the two arrows. The same people you see at the top, you'll see em' at the bottom. Pops, I got em'. I hate that you let that snake kill you. But he got his. A lot of people have got theirs, and I'm guessing that I'm not done yet, either. I need you to watch over me. The police are looking for me, and I need you to guide me through this. Should I kill her, Pops? I know the answer, but it's… it's just hard.

I got mommy into a clinic. She's doing good and will be back in no time. I'll kiss her for you when I see her again. I know you're somewhere calling the shots, being the King. You stay smooth, Pops. And I'ma be out to see you again soon. I love you," I said, then turned and left.

Later on that evening, I pulled into me and Jackie's new estate, and scanned the parking area out front. Jackie's gold Jaguar was parked at the entrance. I pulled behind it and quickly got out the car and raced up the stairs. The front door swung open as I reached the top step. It was Jackie. She was standing there in her silk house coat and slippers. I can tell by the look on her face that something was wrong, but I tried to ignore the look and leaned in to kiss her. Jackie side stepped my kiss, then said.

"Get in here, Coach," she slammed the door behind me.

"Baby, what's wrong. I ain't seen you in two days and I can't get no loving?" I said, standing in the hallway.

"Look at this," Jackie said, slapping me in the chest with a folded newspaper.

I unfolded the paper it was a copy of the Detroit Free Press. On the cover was a picture of the Crew. Somehow they got a picture of me, Nick, Eddie and Black at the Fox Theatre on New Year's Eve. We were each flashing money and had our murder masks on. The headline read: The Crew, wanted for a string of homicides on Detroit's eastside. Then there was a picture of Farwell Park with the police working the crime scene. I scanned the article looking for any mention of witnesses, but none listed.

"So…" Jackie said, cocking her head.

"What? You want me to tell you whether its true or not?" I asked, tossing the paper in a trash can in the corner.

"I deserve that much, don't I?"

"Baby, listen. Don't concern yourself with my affairs. I don't need you worrying."

"Worrying. That's all I've been doing, is in here worrying. I don't want to see you back in jail, Corey" Jackie said, then she began crying.

"Shh… Come here," I said, taking Jackie into my arms. I rubbed Jackie's head while she cried. The word jail was like a dagger through my soul. For me, jail was equal to death.

"Baby, I am not going anywhere. I promise," I said, and I meant every word of it.

*****

While I was in Cleveland, Jackie had ordered all new furniture. She had plushed the whole crib out with fine leather sofas, Persian rugs and all kind of crazy looking artifacts. She even bought a baby Grand piano, which sat dead center of the living room. In all, there were a total of five bathrooms, four full baths, gourmet kitchen with marble counter tops, finished basement equipped with a wet bar and kitchen. Outside sat a guest house with an in-ground swimming pool. Pretty much, it was Caldwell in the suburbs.

I turned the pool house into my office. For the past three days, I had been in there working the phone trying to decipher the business. Word on the street as told to Black, was that Amanda had told police that we kicked her door in and forced her to call Rocko. Then Rocko turned up dead after agreeing to meet me at Farwell school park.

"Word."

"Yeah, man. That's the word. I told you a long time ago when you hit that nucca Deal$ that you shoulda' let me stank the bitch," Black said.

"I know. I fucked up. But uh, any word on where she might be at?"

"I got nuccas scowering the streets now."

"Well, huh, if anything turns up, you kow what to do."

"Without hesitation."

"A'ight. I'ma hit you back in a minute."

"Bet." Click.

My worst fear had been confirmed. Amanda was working with the police, and even worst, she was M.I.A. I had to find the bitch first, and stank her ass like I should have let Black do a long time ago. 'Where could this bitch be hiding?' I sat back in my tall leather chair and kicked my feet up on the desk. The city was big and she could be anywhere. 'Think - Think. How can I smoke this bitch out?' "I got it," I said sitting up in my chair. I snatched the phone off the hook and pushed redial. Black answered on the first ring.

"And while we're at it, put the word out there that it's two hun'd stacks on the demo, and it can be dead or alive."

"Got it," Black said.

I hung the phone up, and kicked my feet back up in the air. "Let's see how long you can hide now, bitch…"

Chapter Fifteen

The Detroit Police Department was so pressed to catch us that they put a $10,000 reward leading to our arrest. I'd seen that shit on the news, and knew we were racing against the clock to find Amanda and stank her ass. It was just a matter of time before someone spotted one of us and called in for that cake…

"Are you sure it's them?"

"Yes, I'm positive. I just served them drinks, and they're sitting right here at the bar," the waitress whispered into the phone,

"Okay, thank you. We're sending someone over there right now." Click. The young waitress had been talking to the police. She called the number listed in the paper for the $10,000 reward. She went back to waiting on customers as if nothing happened.

"Baby, girl. Let me get another double shot of Henny. This round with no ice," Eddie said.

He and Nick were sitting at the bar having a few drinks. They were at Sugar's Sports bar on Chalmers.

"Here you go. Will there be anything else?" asked the waitress, as she set Eddie's drink in front of him.

"Yeah, your phone number," Eddie shot back.

"Before you leave, I'll have it for you," the girl said blushing.

Eddie flirted with her for a moment, then she continued waiting on the other customers.

"You see all that ass on her?" Eddie asked, as he watched ole' girl walk away. Nick hadn't been paying attention. He was turned in the opposite direction. He was mouthing something to three chicks sitting at a table near the window.

"You hear what I said?" Eddie asked, slapping Nick on the back of the head.

"Ah, what?" Nick said, holding his head and turning around to face Eddie. "What?" he asked.

Eddie downed his double shot of Henny, then slammed the empty glass on the counter.

"Nothin'. I'll be back," Eddie said, getting up and heading for the restroom.

Nick slid off his stool and walked over to where the three ladies were sitting. "How ya'll lovely ladies doing? Mind if I buy ya'll a drink?" Nick asked.

"That's cool. Have a seat," one of the chicks said.

Nick took a seat next to the girl he had been eyeing. "And what's yo' name?" asked Nick.

"Michelle."

"I know who you are. Your White boy Nick, from the Crew," the girl across from Nick said.

Nick was smiling from ear to ear and hadn't seen the four narcos step into the bar. They scanned the floor, then one of them pointed toward Nick who's back was to the door,

"What the fuck?" Nick said, as two narco's snatched him out of his chair from behind. Then took him to the floor, pinning their knees in his back, then cuffed him. "Stand him up," ordered one of the narcs.

The two dick suckas pulled Nick to his feet.

"Where's your partner?" the head narc asked Nick.

Eddie was on his way out the bathroom and peeped game. He and Nick locked eyes and the narc who'd been questioning Nick saw how Nick eyes shifted. He turned around and caught four hot ones to the chest. Boom! Boom! Boom! Boom! Eddie had pulled his hoody down over his eyes to conceal his identity. He was side stepping toward the front still bustin'. Boom! Boom!

One of the cops detained Nick, while the other two drew their gun's and gave chase after Eddie who was out the door.

"Officer down, shots fired. Officer down," the narc reported over his radio before exiting Sugar's. Boom!

Boom! Boom! Eddie shot three times nearly hitting the second narc as he was coming out behind his partner.

Boom! Boom! The first narc returned fire, while his partner scrambled to safety behind a white Ford Taurus. Eddie was at the trunk of the Maseretti, he knew it was a matter of minutes before more police would be on the scene and it was now or never. The two were positioned to where they had Eddie boxed in, they were crunched over behind two cars near the entrance/exit. They tried stalling Eddie until back up arrived, letting off a series of rounds. Boom! Boom! Eddie came out the trunk with a fully auto AR-15, it's 50 round clip was flipped with body armor piercing wolf head bullets.

"You bitches wanna hide, huh?" Eddie said stepping into the middle of the parking lot, letting the AR ride out. Laaka... Laaka... Laaka... He hit the narc who was hiding behind the white Taurus in the neck twice. A series of bullets went through the cars quarter panel at a downward angle and came out through the trunk where the narc was crunched over. He fell over and died instantly. Eddie could hear sirens in the distance, he back stepped still shooting. He struck the second narc in the thigh, then shoulder putting him out of commission.

Laaka! Laaka! Laaka! Eddie let off a few more rounds just for measure, then jumped behind the wheel of his Maseretti, and peeled off. As he was flying down Chalmers, squad cars with their lights on were heading in the direction of Sugar's. He passed them doing a buck and some change. Seeing the lights in the rear-view mirror, all he could think about was Nick...

<u>1300 Beaubien, Detroit Police Headquarters</u>

Downtown Detroit, Nick sat on the 9th floor of the 1st precinct inside an interrogation room. He was seated dead center of the floor in a steel chair staring into the two-way glass that separated him and the detectives behind it.

"This scrony piece of shit is White boy Nick?" The one from the Crew, who's everyone screaming his fuckin' name like he's a damn celebrity?" asked the lead detective Roy Hazelwood. He was staring Nick back in the eyes from behind the two-way glass.

"That's the one," answered Hazelwood's partner, Detective Christine Burgerhof. She was a red head broad. She'd just transferred in from Boston. She and Hazelwood had become partners days before. The Crew's case would be their first assignment together, and Hazelwood was determined not to blow it. It was his big break…

"Listen, when we get in there, let me handle this chump," said Hazelwood. He was a middle-aged white man. Bad body built, and going bald.

Hazelwood swung the door open to the interrogation room, letting the knob slam hard against the back wall. He stormed into the room with Burgerhof in tow. "You little fuck!" yelled Hazelwood, grabbing Nick by the throat with one hand. Hazelwood stood Nick up, more like raised him up by choking him. Nick was turning red, 'cause his wind pipe had been cut off.

Burgerhof was starting to worry. She nudged her partner to cool it. "Sit him back in his chair," she said, holding Hazelwood's arm. Little did she know, that was exactly what Hazelwood expected her to do, play the savior. Good cop, bad cop so to speak. Stepping back and releasing Nick, Hazelwood huffed and puffed as if he were the one who'd just been choked.

Nick was still handcuffed behind his back, so there wasn't much he could do besides take the ill treatment, and just hope they didn't hurt him too badly.

"Where are they?" demanded Hazelwood.

Nick was still coughing. He wasn't moving as fast as Hazelwood wanted him too.

"You hear me, shit face?" Hazelwood back slapped Nick out of his chair.

Burgerhof, held Hazelwood off, while Nick gained his composure.

"I suggest you start talking, or I swear to God," said Hazelwood.

Nick got up, then took his seat. He looked Hazelwood square in the face, then said. "You swear what? That shoulda' been your pig ass back there laying dead with…"

Before Nick could finish his sentence, ole' Hazelwood tackled him to the floor. He started banging Nick's head against the tile floor. "You worthless fucker!" yelled Hazelwood, while he continued to bang Nick's head. "I'll fuckin' kill your ass."

Burgerhof tried to stop the assault, but Hazelwood pushed her away. He started punching Nick in the face. He didn't stop swinging until both Nick's eyes were swollen and closed shut. Nick's mouth and nose were busted.

Hazelwood stood to his feet, then planted his boot in Nick's rib cage.

"Ahh!" screamed Nick in agony.

"No one's going to come save your lousy ass. Get up," said Hazelwood, snatching Nick from the floor like a rag doll. He raced Nick over to an open window facing Beaubien Street. He stuck Nick half way out of the window. "You think you can fly?" asked Hazelwood. They were staring down nine stories. "I can throw your ass outta this window, and cover it up. So, I suggest you start talking," said Hazelwood.

"Get your hands off of my client," said Mr. Davidson, stepping into the room.

Detective Hazelwood reluctantly pulled Nick from the window. Nick didn't know how lucky he was Mr. Davidson had shown up. A moment more, and he'd been dead.

Chapter Sixteen

"What? Where at?"

"Up at Sugar's."

"What the fuck was he doing at Sugar's? I told that nucca to stay outta them fuckin' bars. Where's Eddie?"

"He's right here."

"Ya'll nuccas get out here, now?" I yelled, slamming the phone down. Black had just advised me of what happed with Nick and Eddie. There it was, all over the News. I turned up the TV mounted on my wall inside the master bath. I was soaking in a hot bath with Jackie. I caught the tail end of the story.

"Cops say that they are in desperate need of your help in the apprehension of these three men, the other ¾'s of the infamous Crew. Again one detective shot dead, and two others listed in serious condition. Police believe this man is responsible for the shooting. If you have any information, please call police. I'm Monica Maham…"

I cut the TV off, then leaned back into the bubble bath.

"Why do they keep flashing your picture every time something in the city happens?" asked Jackie.

She was lying across my chest.

"They're trying to paint me as the bad guy," I said.

"Let me take some of the stress away, baby," Jackie said, then disappeared under the bubbles. She was skulling me up under water. She must have had gills hidden somewhere, cause she stayed under there until she got what she was looking for, a nut.

"Ahh…" I closed my eyes and waited until I heard a knock on the door from Black and Eddie.

*****

"Eddie, what happened?" I asked. Black, Eddie and I were down in my basement. I was standing behind the bar fixing Eddie and Black some drinks. I was coming outta the bathroom…"

I cut Eddie off. "No, I mean what happened to what I said. Staying outta the bars? Remember that?" I said slamming my hand down on the bar counter.

Eddie just dropped his head. "I know, I fucked up," he said.

"You damn right, you fucked up. You're bigger than that, E. You let Nick's freaky ass talk you into stepping off in Sugar's. I can see him now, selling you a dream about all the hoes that was gonna be in there. You know how Nick thinks with his dick. Now we got even more heat on us," I said, turning on the News. "Look at that shit. It's been on all day. The whole city is lookin' for us. And since one of theirs is dead, ya'll already know they got the green light to kill our ass on sight. And even worse, they got Nick. Damn!" I yelled.

"Yeah, they probably got Nick downtown at 1300 torturing the shit out of his ass," Black said.

"Betta know it. But Nick's solid, he won't break. I got Mr. Davidson on his way down there right now to stop any further interrogation," I said.

"So, what can we do right now? You know, to help Nick?" asked Eddie.

"The best thing you can do right now is lay low. I want you and Black to take a trip outta town. Leave the city. Go somewhere, anywhere. Trust me, the city will be here when you get back."

I picked up the phone on the wall, and called Jackie upstairs. "Baby, get me two tickets to Lexington, Kentucky. The next thing smoking. Nah, better yet don't worry about it."

"Are you sure, Corey?" I can do that with no problem," Jackie said.

"Yeah, I'm sure," I said, hanging up the phone. I had forgotten that we were national criminals. Black and Eddie's face were all over the News. I couldn't have them walking through no airport. They'd be in cuffs before they even boarded the plane.

'Think-Think.' I told myself. I picked up the phone and called Torch…

"I appreciate it. A'ight, Torch. They'll be there in an hour," I said, hanging up the phone.

"Who the fuck is Torch?" asked Black.

"Never mind that, my nucca. Look, I just booked ya'll a private flight out to Lexington. I already holla'd at Shawanna the lil' stripper bitch, and she said ya'll can stay with her. But I suggest ya'll rent a room, and just have her show ya'll around."

"Why you sending us to Kentucky?" asked Eddie.

"Cause when I asked you where you wanted to go, you didn't know. And I figured that, because all yo' life you've been stuck in Detroit. In times like these, we gotta move around. Plus ya'll can meet some new contacts for when all this blows over. Come on, I'ma have Jackie drive ya'll to the airport."

"And what about you, Coach, what you gonna do?" asked Black.

"It's my fault this is all happening to begin with. So, I'ma be the one to fix it…."

I gave Eddie and Black a duffle bag with $250,000 in it. We hit rocks and hugged, as I saw them off with Jackie to the airport…

Chapter Seventeen

I had to hit the city and move around if I were going to find Amanda, and save Nick from a life sentence. I couldn't risk driving through the city. I'd be right beside Nick at 1300 Beaubien. I called my man Miles and had him send a limousine to pick me up.

I rode down 7 Mile taking in all the hustlin' and bustlin' going down from behind the comfort of the limo's tinted windows. The limo stopped at a red light on 7 Mile and Van Dyke, we pulled alongside a police cruiser. I stared the young white office riding shotgun in his face. He looked at my window, but couldn't see my face. I smiled as the light turned green and traffic began moving.

"Only if you knew who was behind this tint, bitch," I said.

We continued down 7 Mile, driving east. "Pull over at the curb right here," I told the driver. The limo parked in front of Fatt Mark's Barber shop on Norwood. I picked up the phone between the consoles and dialed the number painted on the building.

"Coach?" Mark said.

"Come outside," I said.

Mark hung up the phone, and excused himself from the guy whose hair he'd been cutting. He stepped out the barber shop and looked east to west. Not paying attention to the black Lincoln limo parked at the curb. Mark scratched his head.

I rolled the window down half way, and whistled. Mark locked eyes with me, then smiled. I scooted over as Mark headed for the door.

"What's good, my nucca?" Mark said, climbing into the limo. We embraced for a moment, then Mark looked at me and said, "Man, ya'll nuccas is hot as E-mothafucka."

"I know. Driver, pull off," I said. The limo pulled into traffic, and I poured myself and Mark a drink. Mark had been my barber since back in the day. He was a retired hustla who was getting that legit money now. He was good friends with King David, and was known to be a loyal nucca, which was why I was seeking his help. He kept his ear to the street, even though he wasn't in the game no more. I knew if anybody knew where Amanda was hiding, it was Mark. The barber shop always had the word.

"Mark, I need your help on something," I said.

"Anything for you, Coach, man. What's up?"

"I'm tryna' find that chick, Amanda. You know the one who got the whole Detroit Police Department looking for me? Have you heard anything?"

"Yeah. And I can tell you right now that it ain't gonna be easy, but it can be done," Mark said, before downing his drink.

I was on the edge of my seat. "Where is she?" I asked, with eyes bucked.

"They got the bitch under witness protection. They want ya'll so bad, that they're going to buy her a house and give her $50,000 for testifying. Right now she could be anywhere. I got a man though, downtown. For the right price, he could lead you right to her."

"You know I gotta lot of problems, Mark, but money ain't one of em'. Whatever dude wants, tell em' to name his price and he got that."

Mark picked up the car phone and dialed a number. "Yeah, Gabe. It's me, Mark. I need to locate the whereabouts of someone ya'll got put away. You know the demo from the Crew's case…Uh, huh. Stacks are on deck. I will take care of it. Okay." He's got me on hold," Mark whispered. "Yeah, I know where it is. Okay. Stop by the shop later on, and I'll have that for you." Click…

"What's the ticket?" I asked.

"He wants $20,000," Mark said, but I'll take care of it, and you just get me back whenever you can."

"So, where is she?" I asked.

"She's at the Renaissance Hotel on Jefferson."

"A'ight, I'll just go in there and kick the door in, then blow the bitch brains out."

"I told you it wasn't going to be easy. Not that easy, anyway. They got around the clock police on the bitch. Four of em', two inside the room and two outside. It can be done, but i'ts gonna take some serious planning. And most importantly, it's gonna take some nuts…"

"Yeah," I said, staring off into space. I had sent Black and Eddie to Kentucky. I knew they would have gotten the job done. I took a deep breath, and then exhaled slowly. 'I gotta get this shit done,' I thought.

"What room is she in?" I asked.

"1232 on the tenth floor. Look, Coach, if you need some help with the job, I got the right men for you, but it's gonna cost," Mark said.

"I just might need em'," I said, fixing myself another drink. I downed the glass of Crown Royal, then sat back and fired up a blunt of Gran's. "Yeah, I just might need em'." I blew out a cloud of smoke, then passed the L to Mark.

"Driver, take us back to the barber shop," I ordered.

"Mark, you think you can get me five men?" I asked, as a plan came to me.

"No problem. When you want em'?" Mark asked.

"Tonight. But I need five men who don't know who I am."

"That's gonna be hard, but I think I can pull it off. I got some good men from the Chi. They're GD's."

"A'ight, well I'ma go get ready, how long you think it'll take em' to get here?" I asked, as we pulled in front of the barber shop.

"It'll take about three hours to get here."

"A'ight. I'll be back before then," I said, giving Mark some dap. He climbed out the limo, and I instructed the driver to drive on.

"Pull over right here," I said. The driver parked in front of the Post Office on 7 Mile and Caldwell. "Leave the engine running I'll be back in a minute," I told the driver.

I put my hoody over my head, then climbed out of the limo. I cut across the street and turned into the alley making sure no one had seen me. I walked down three blocks through the alley and crossed Hillsdale onto my block. I ducked low at the entrance of the Pit-bull farm and scanned the yard for anything unusual. Everything seemed to be normal, nothing was out of place. So, I jumped the privacy fence into my backyard, and crept up to the sliding door leading into the kitchen. I slid inside the house and tip toed into the living room. I inspected every room and saw that no one had been in there since the last time the Crew had left. I grabbed a green duffle bag out of the bedroom closet, then walked into King David's library. I pulled the Art of War from the shelf, then flicked the switch on the wall. The wall did a 180° turn revealing King David's armory.

I filled the bag with 6 AR-15's with the short stock's making them easy to conceal. I grabbed ten extra clips, then flipped the wall back around. With the bag over my shoulder, I locked up the house, and took the alley back up to 7 Mile. I crossed the street in a hurry and climbed into the back of the limo.

"Pull off," I told the driver.

"Where to, sir?" asked the driver.

"Just cruise around. I'll let you know when I need to make a stop," I said.

I needed some time to just think. I fixed myself a double shot of Crown Royal, then sat back in my seat. 'This shit is gonna have to go down smooth. One wrong move, and it could cost everyone involved their life,' I thought. I just hoped the men Mark had for me were some ridas…

Chapter Eighteen

I looked at my watch, and it was time to meet Mark at the shop. His guys should be pulling up any minute. I instructed the driver to go back to the barber shop. I was putting the final touches on my master plan, when the limo pulled in front of the barber shop. I could see several nuccas inside the shop through the window, men I had never seen before. I called into the shop, and I saw Mark look out at the limo.

"Come on, that's him outside," Mark said.

The five men inside followed Mark outside. I popped the locks and they all got in the limo behind Mark.

"Aye, y' all this is my man. He wishes not to state his name, but I assure you he's good people. He needs your help on some thangs of you all's interest. I'ma let y'all chop it up on the specifics," Mark said.

I hit rocks with all of them, no one stating any names, which was cool with me. I preferred it that way. I got straight down to business, enlightening them on my plan…

"That sound like some shit straight out of a movie," one of them nuccas said. They all started laughing and shit, but I was dead ass serious.

"Look, Joe," the leader of the pack said, "The shit sounds hella crazy, but that's what we do for a living. We make movies. So, if that's how you wanna rock it, let's go." We hit rocks, then I hit rocks with the other four…

"Y'all ready?" I asked.

"Let's get it," one of em' said.

"That's my cue to bounce. Ya'll nuccas be careful, and get it done," Mark said, giving us all dap before climbing out the limo.

I instructed the driver as to where our next stop would be. "The Renaissance Center," I said.

I unzipped the green duffle bag sitting between my legs, then handed each of them an AR-15 and two extra clips.

"This that boy, right here," one of em' said, holding his AR up and looking at it.

I fired up an L, and took a long pull. I was trying to get my head right for what lied ahead…

The limo pulled in front of the Renaissance Center, and parked directly across the street from the towers, where the buildings were located. I looked at all the people coming

and leaving from the building from the back window of the limo.
"We're going in there?" one of the nuccas asked, looking up at the two towers.
"It's a whole lot of mothafuckas out here," another one said.
The leader of the pack looked at me and said, "Look, Joe, like I told you before, me and my men are with you a hun'd percent. I just hope you got us a way outta there."
Truth was, I didn't. I couldn't guarantee the nucca that everybody was gonna make it out in one piece. That's what the AR-15's was for. A nucca was gone have to shoot his way out. But I wasn't about to tell them that. I told myself, 'fuck these out of town ass nuccas.' My loyalty was to Nick, Black, Eddie and myself. As long as I made it out, and the job got done, that was all that mattered to me.
"Here's what we gonna do," I said, before taking the last hit on my blunt, then flicking it out the window. "Y'all two, your job is to secure the lobby. If any police enter the building, lay their asses out. However, in the midst of us handling our business, y'all just chill and try to blend in with the people in the lobby. And me and you, we gonna play the diversion," I said talking to the leader. "Soon as we hit, ya'll two hit," I said.

"I told you that shit sounds like a movie," Dawg said laughing.

"Well, then action," I said, climbing out the limo.

Dawg and I entered the hotel first, while the other four broke off into pairs. I walked up to the counter and asked the woman working where the kitchen for room service was located. I told her that I had a complaint and wanted to report it personally.

"Around the corner and down the hall to your left," she informed.

"Thank you," I said, as me and Dawg fell into step.

We reached the end of the hall, stopping in front of the two stainless steel swinging doors. We looked around, then pushed through the kitchen doors on a straight mission. The scene couldn't have been more perfect. There were two white boys loading silver food trays and pushing carts. They hadn't noticed me and Dawg entering the kitchen, because they had their backs to us. I looked at Dawg and nodded to the one at his right.

"He looks about your size," I said.

Dawg nodded, then pulled his AR-15 from the inside of his coat.

I simultaneously reached for my AR, as I headed in the other white boy's direction. I poked him in his back with the nose of my rifle, and he turned around nearly shitting on himself. His eyes bucked wide open, as I came down over his head with the butt end of my rifle. His body slumped to the ground. I looked over and Dawg had his man knocked out too.

"Come on, drag these bitches in the freezer before somebody come," I said, grabbing ole' boy by his ankles and dragging him into the meat freezer. We stripped they asses out of their work uniforms and left em' knocked out in their drawers.

"We can't leave em' like that. They gonna wake up in a minute," Dawg said.

"Yeah, you right," I said, scanning the kitchen. I saw a huge roll of plastic mounted on this machine. I guess they used it to wrap up meat, so they could store it. 'Perfect,' I thought, racing over to get the plastic. "Help me pull this roll off," I said.

We put them two Yankees backs to each other, then wrapped their asses up about a thousand times in plastic, head and all. Dawg looked at em' on the way out the freezer, before closing the door and said, "Now ya'll gon' be fresh to death."

I laughed. "You's a fool, man. Come on," I said.

In our borrowed uniforms, we pushed the two carts of food the white boys had been loading. We pushed them out into the hallway and casually bent the corner passing the front desk heading for the elevators. When I hit the up button for the elevators, everybody was in position, the two men who were to hit the room first were tucked low at the back of the elevator.

"Nice outfits," one of them said, as Dawg and I pushed the carts onto the elevator.

"Tenth floor," I said.

Everyone knew their role. There was no need to talk. The elevator door opened, stopping on the tenth floor, and I led the way pushing my cart. As we bent the corner, we could see two plain-clothed cops sitting in two chairs down the hall. Dawg and I fell into step; he lined his cart up with mine and headed in the cop's direction.

Ding! I heard the elevator ring. That meant our men were right behind us.

"Let's make a movie," Dawg whispered, as we brought our carts to a stop in front of the two officers.

"Room service for 232," I said looking at the room number on the door. "Anybody order room service?" asked one of the cops. He stood up. He was an old bald-headed fat white guy who looked like he should be on desk duty. His partner was a skinny young black kid. He looked like he was fresh out of the academy.

"I don't know, but it sure smells good," the young one said, standing.

"What is it?" asked the fat one. He leaned his nose down over the cart.

Dawg and I pulled the covers off the serving trays, and came up blasting... Laaka! Laaka!... I hit the old fat man in the top of his head about five times before his body hit the floor. I stood over him and aired his ass out. Laaka! Laaka!... I shot him four more times in the face, splattering brain matter all over the carpet and walls.

Dawg was handling the youngster. He flat lined his ass with a series of shots to the face and chest. He lay slumped over dead next to his partner with half his face missing. I turned and looked at the sound of gun shots. Boom! Boom! Laaka! Laaka! Boom! The door to the room was wide open, and our men were in. Boom! Boom! Laaka! Laaka! More shots licked off. Dawg and I got low, hunched over we entered the battlefield. One of our men was crunched behind a wooden table. He had it flipped onto its side, using it as a shield.

Laaka! Laaka! I let off two shots in the direction of a cop who was hiding on the side of the door frame leading into the bathroom. Boom! Boom! Boom! The cop returned fire on me and Dawg as we ran toward the flipped table where my man was crunched over. Boom! Boom! Two shots ripped through the table, both shots hitting Dawg in the shoulder.

"Fuck!" Dawg yelled. He wasn't wearing a vest. Boom! Boom! Boom! The cop caught the other nucca trying to peek his head up. He hit the nucca dead center mask. His head jerked back like he'd broken his neck, then his body fell backwards crashing to the floor.

'We target practice behind this table,' I thought. I stood up busting wildly at the door frame. Laaka! Laaka! Boom! The cop returned fire, planting a single round into my bulletproof vest. I fanned his ass out through the wall. Laaka! I rushed into the living room and the room was empty, with the exception of our other man. He laid dead in the middle of the floor, with his face down and blood pouring out his scalp. There was a door on the wall leading into the next room. It was wide opened. I crept through the next room and it was all empty. "Damn," I said. The bitch had got away… I walked back into the room where Dawg was at. He was still behind the table, bleeding badly. "You gotta get me to the hospital," he said clutching his shoulder.

"That won't be necessary," I said raising my AR-15 to Dawg's head. Laaka! Laaka! Two head shots put him to rest. I tucked my AR-15 into my pants and took off the room service coat. I threw the coat down and stepped into the hall as if nothing happened. People were coming out of the rooms now that the smoke had cleared. I put my head to the floor avoiding eye contact with the nosy residents. I turned the corner down a hall where no one seemed to care about the latest events. I broke into a full speed spring stopping at the stairs.

I ran down the ten flights, then stopped at the ground floor door. I took two deep breaths, then stepped into the hall. Laaka! Laaka! Shots rang out as I turned into the lobby. I reached for my AR, but didn't pull it. The two men I had posted in the lobby was getting it in. They were dropping police left and right as they tried to enter the hotel doors. Laaka! Laaka! Laaka!

"That's right, hold em' off," I said, turning on my heels.

I walked hastily down the hall and turned into the baggage room. I walked past all the workers while they handed customers' luggage. There was a door leading to the back dock, it was wide open. The light beaming outside the door from the street lights, seemed like the light of heaven as I walked through the door and out into the alley way. I picked up my step to a light sprint reaching the front entrance of the hotel. I looked both ways, then crossed the street heading for the limo. I climbed into the back of the limo and told the driver to pull off. "Take me home," I said, as we pulled away from the curb. In the distance, I could still hear gun shots.

I fixed myself a glass of Crown Royal, then sat back in my seat. I took a sip from my glass, then said. "Yeah, you got away bitch. But you won't be so lucky next time. I promise…

Chapter Nineteen

Back to the drawing board, I thought, as I paced the floor of the pool house. Last night was a complete disaster. The only thing I did was tip the police off that I wanted Amanda dead. Now they would hide the bitch even better, and worst for the Crew, more heat would come our way.

"Baby, Mr. Davidson is here to see you," Jackie said, knocking on the pool house door.

"Thank you baby," I said, as my lawyer Mr. Davidson walked into the pool house.

"Corey. I had no idea you were doing this well for yourself. I'ma have to start charging you more," Mr. Davidson joked.

"How are you, sir?" I asked, shaking his hand.

"I should be asking you that question. Do you know how bad the city of Detroit wants you off the street?" Mr. Davidson asked.

"Yeah, I know," I said stepping behind the bar and pouring myself a drink. "You want one?" I asked.

"You got any Scotch?" asked Mr. Davidson.

I pulled a brand new bottle of Scotch off the shelf and handed it to him. He poured himself a glass, downed it, and then poured another."You know the FBI is looking to get involved."

"What?" I asked.

"After last night's blood bath, they don't know if the locals can handle the Crew. I mean, assuming that that's who's responsible for the mayhem."

"So, what does that mean if the FBI gets involved? What will be the difference?"

"More man power for one, which also means more exposure, like America's Most Wanted. You'll be on every Saturday special alerting our entire nation. Millions of people will know who you are, what you look like. You won't be able to leave your house. Hell, your neighbors might see your picture and call it in. See, right now it's local. No one really cares what happens to the inner city. However, when hotels such as the Renaissance, are no longer a safe place for the corporate folks and tourists, the big guns come out. You have to remember, it's all about politics and money, just like in your world."

"So, what about my man Nick, what they holding him on?"

"They're holding him on the strength of you, and the recent events. I went down to see him yesterday."

"How's he doing?"

"Besides the two black eyes and broken ribs, he's doing fine. I had the sergeant move him to a more secure part of the jail, where there are cameras. That way the police can't jump him anymore without supervision, you know how they do?"

"What's it gonna to take to get him out?"

"For you to succeed in what was attempted last night, the next time you try. Without the girl, the State doesn't have a case," Mr. Davidson said, then gulped his drink. He was down with the street-code. He hated rats, and felt like they should be slaughtered. Mr. Davidson was the truth. He represented all the old mobsters in Detroit back in the day. They called him, "Don't Sweat it Davidson," because that's what he'd tell all his clients. Don't sweat it…

It was hard not to sweat this one, though. It wasn't looking too good for the home team.

"But how am I going to find the bitch now? There ain't no telling where they're hiding her ass out. And wherever they have her, best believe they got the S.W.AT. guarding her," I said.

"You better know it," Mr. Davidson said, taking a sip from his freshly fixed Scotch.

"Do you mind?" I asked, before lighting the blunt I had been rolling.

"Go ahead, just don't hit it all," said Mr. Davidson.

I fired up the L and took two hard pulls. I let the smoke out over my head, while contemplating my next move. I had nothing.

"Help me out here. I can't come up with anything," I said passing the L to Mr. Davidson.

"See one thing about you, Mr. D, I know how bad you hate losing. And I know that you'll do anything to win, so what I'm asking you is for you to give me some advice. How would the mob handle this?"

Mr. Davidson passed me the blunt back. His face was beat red 'cause he was choking on the smoke…

"What the hell is that shit?" he asked wiping his face. "You're tryna' kill me?" he said.

I couldn't help but laugh. I knew his ass was gonna choke out when he hit them good Gan's. He must've thought it was some regulars.

Mr. Davidson took a sip from his Scotch, then cleared his throat.

"You have to pay attention to detail, Corey," he began. "You see, it's like a game of chess. You're trying to capture the king too quickly. In order to get the king, you have to go through his army. And this case is no different. The king happens to be the most vulnerable piece on the board besides the pawn. It can only move one square at a time, which is what makes it so weak. You remove the pieces around it from the board, and check mate."

I had never played chess a day in my life, so all that talk went over my head. I was waiting for Mr. Davidson to stop talking in parabols, and just give me the play.

"Her kids, Corey. You get her by getting her kids," Mr. Davidson said, breaking the silence between us.

"They've got them in witness protection, though," I said. "How am I going to get them?"

"What month is it, Corey?"

"April," I answered.

"And what month does school let out?"

"In June."

"Exactly. Those kids are attending someone's school somewhere I doubt she's smart enough to homeschool them. Every day, Monday through Friday they're getting up and going to school.

"You're an old brilliant, evil son of a bitch," I said smiling.

"So, as long as you know it, I won't have to kill you. Give me a few days and I'll have the name and location of the school for you," Mr. Davidson said. "Now give me some of the weed to take home with me. The wife is going to love it."

I gave Mr. Davidson an ounce of Gan. And then we put the finishing touches on our plan. We dubbed the mission, operation snatch…

Chapter Twenty

While Mr. Davidson was doing what he do, finding out what school Amanda's boys were attending, I thought it would be a good idea to take a trip and get away from the city for a while. Jackie was mad as hell I wasn't taking her with me. I told her it was strictly business, but the truth is, I was on my way to Lexington to surprise Black and Eddie. I missed the shit out of them nuccas.

I had Torch fly me on his private jet. He had asked me about Nick, and I couldn't even look him in the eyes. I did assure him that I was doing everything to get Nick home. But Torch understood, he was in the life of crime himself. Shit, he was a Hells Angels member. He knew how the game went, jail came with it.

Torch dropped me off at this little private airfield, we shook hands and he was back in the sky. I took a taxi to the address Shawanna had given me over the phone. We pulled in front of an old dusty green bungalow style house. I paid the driver and told him to wait, because from the looks of the house, I wasn't about to be laying up in there. I rang the door bell to the house, and the door swung open. It was Black. His eyes bucked like he'd seen a demon.

"Coach! My nucca," Black said, opening his arms to hug me. We embraced for a moment. I waved the cab to go on.

"What you doing out here my nucca, how come you ain't call and let us know you were coming?"

"I wanted to surprise ya'll. What up, doe?"

"Man, I'm ready to get the fuck back to the city. It's slow as shit out here. And they got this dirt ass weed out here."

"I got something for that ass," I said digging into my Louis Vutton bag.

"Please let it be them Gan's," Black said, crossing his fingers.

I pulled up a pound of nothing but Gan's. Black damn near shit on himself when I handed him the ziploc bag.

"Where E-double at?" I asked.

"Come on. You can wake his ass up," Black said, leading me into the house.

Chicken heads filled the living room, they all were eyeing me and cheesin', showing their gold teeth as Black led me past them and into the back hall. I thought I had seen something dart across the floor as we passed the bathroom. I stopped in my tracks spotting a huge cock roach on the wall. "Black," I whispered, pointing to the roach. "I thought I told y'all to get a room."

"You act like you ain't never had roaches, nucca, come on," Black said, leading the way. He must've forgotten that growing up, my crib was always clean. King David wasn't having that shit. Black's crib was the one that had mice and roaches. We pushed open the door to the back bedroom. Eddie was sprawled out across the bed on his stomach sleeping with his mouth open. The room had a musty smell, like somebody had just finished fucking. The fan perched inside the window pane wasn't helping the stench much. I looked around at all the dirty clothes that lined the floor and decorated the dresser. Sanford and Son was playing on an aged 20" Zenith TV. The set was so old that the color was bleeding, and at the top of the screen, was a bunch of black lines.

"Ya'll nuccas living foul as shit," I said.

"You gonna wake the nucca up, or you want me to do it?" Black asked.

For real, I was scared to touch anything. Even the sheets on the bed were filthy. Eddie had one hand tossed over the back of a female lying next to him. She had a cover over her face, so I couldn't tell who the woman was. Black reached down and snatched the sheet off Eddie and the woman who both sat up.

"Nucca, what the fuck?" Eddie snapped on Black.

I stepped from behind Black, and Eddie's face lit up.

"My nucca?" he jumped out of bed wrapping his arms around my neck.

"Telll me you here to get us," Eddie said, excitedly as if it were a question.

"Yeah, sorta, something like that. But we gonna chill for a few days. Y'all nuccas show me the town. You know, just kick it," I said, looking into the woman's eyes who had been lying beside Eddie. It was Shawanna's car hopping ass.

"You ain't gone say hi?" Shawanna said getting out of bed ass naked.

"What's up lil' moma, you miss me?" I asked smiling. "You know I brought you something."

"What is it?" Shawanna asked, as she walked over and gave me a hug. I palmed both her ass cheeks and played with the pussy from the back.

"What you bring me?" she asked.

"You know all I got is a hard dick and bubble gum, baby," I said.

Shawanna hit me on the shoulder.

"Let me get dressed," Shawanna said, then walked out of the room.

"So, what's the deal? Is everything straight, when can we go home?" asked Eddie.

"Hell nah, it ain't straight," I said.

"What's up with Nick?" asked Black.

"They're still holding him on some conspiracy shit. Mr. Davidson went to see him. He said they broke his ribs and gave him two black eyes."

"I say we just run up in that bitch and get him up outta there," Eddie said.

"Trust me, if it were that easy you know it would be done, but it's a lot more complicated than that, which is why I came to get y'all. We're gonna have to strap up one more time. We gotta do it for Nick," I said.

"I don't know what made you think you was get it done without us anyway. Nucca, you know we like the A-Team," Eddie said, smiling.

"Yeah, and yo' crazy ass is Murdock," Black said. We all bust out laughing…

"But nah, seriously though, man, I'm not closing my eyes in this rat shack. Take me to get a room," I said.

"A lil' dirt ain't never hurt nobody. It's good for the soul, it keeps you grounded," Black said.

"You just gonna make that shit make sense, huh? Man take me to get a room," I said, laughing.

"Where y'all going?" Shawanna asked, stepping out of the bathroom.

We were at the end of the hall and Black and Eddie had their coats on.

"We 'bouts to take Coach to the Regency, so he can get a room," answered Black.

"What, you too good to stay in my house?" asked Shawanna.

"Nah, it ain't like that. I just ain't tryna' impose on you. And it's a lil' crowded in here, but why don't you come with me?" I said.

"Oh, I was gonna do that anyway," Shawanna said. 'Hold on, let me grab my purse."

"Why you tell her where we were going? You know it's gonna be hard to shake her ass. Plus, I was tryna' fuck with them new hoes we met at the Derby," Eddie said.

"What the fuck is a Derby?" I asked.

"Long story," Eddie said.

"Fuck y'all nuccas been up to out here?" I laughed.

"I'm ready," Shawanna said, stepping into the hall.

"Where y'all going?" one of the gold teeth chicken heads asked, as we walked through the living room.

"None of yo' damn business," Shawanna snapped.

Good, I thought. I wasn't trying to be around them funky bitches. I was gonna throw my clothes away, as soon as we checked into the hotel. We all packed into Shawanna's lil' red two door Ford Fiesta. The car was so small my knees were in my chest riding in the back seat with Shawanna. It made it hard for her to get my whole dick in her mouth. She sucked at the head, while Black and Eddie got their lungs out of the street. Them nuccas had six blunts in rotation, and it was only four people in the car.

We checked into the Regency Hotel, downtown on Rosa Parks Ave. across from the University of Kentucky. Nothing but country-fed, thick white girls filled the lobby of the hotel. Damn, why I bring this bitch with me? I cursed myself as I took in all the eye-candy.

"Just like a nucca. Get a lil' money, and you wanna try everything new," Shawanna said, grabbing my hand as to claim me. "Come on," she said, leading me towards the elevator.

Black and Eddie were giving me the pinky wave good-bye. Shawanna and I rode the elevator up to the sixth floor, then stepped off. Our room was 318, which was just two doors down. As soon as we hit the door, Shawanna went to tearing at my clothes, lifting my shirt over my head and pulling my pants down. She fell to her knees and slapped my stiff dick in her mouth. My knees started buckling from Shawanna's platinum head game. She hit me off with no hands and just the right amount of spit. She let my dick slide out of her mouth, letting it slap her in the face as it yearned for her sucking.

Shawanna teased the head of my dick with her tongue ring, wrapping the ball of the ring around my head in soft circles. I stood her up and escorted her into the bathroom. I wanted some of that fire pussy, but first, I was going to scrub Shawanna's ass clean. I ran a bath and poured some bubble bath in the water, while Shawanna stripped down. Holding her by the hand, I helped her into the water. I was still standing on the outside of the tub. Shawanna was looking at me, like 'ain't you gonna join me.'

I grabbed a scrub brush off the counter, then dipped it in the soap suds and started scrubbing the dirt off Shawanna's ass.

"You got jokes, huh?" She had the nerve to fix her lips and say.

"Nah, I was tryna' be romantic, and give you a bath," I lied.

I kept scrubbing her ass as if she were a dog. I pulled her out of the water and rolled a condom back on my dick. Soaking wet, I bent her over the sink and packed my dick in her ass hole. Shawanna waled like she was being murdered.

"Ahh! Ahh!..." she moaned, while looking me in my eyes through the mirror mounted above the sink.

Hearing her moan, only made me thrust harder and faster. I was long dickin' her lil' ass, hitting bottoms with every stroke.

I pulled out of Shawanna, and went over to the cabinet to get a towel. The condom had busted 'cause I was hitting it too hard. While I was washing my dick off, I heard Black and Eddie enter the room.

"Where yall at?" hollered Eddie.

Black came walking into the bathroom. He had this devilish smirk on his face as he eyed the shit out of Shawanna's naked body. She was sitting on the toilet with her legs bust wide open and pussy hanging over the seat. I could tell by the way Shawanna was acting that Black had hit the pussy before.

"Come on, let's show Coach how we been doing it," Black said, as he unfastened his pants, then pulled his dick through this boxers. He slapped that boy straight in Shawanna's mouth and she went to work as if I weren't even standing there. That shit wasn't nothing. We done bust down too many hoes together. We were on some playa' shit for real. As long as it wasn't our main bitch, we were setting hoes out, no matter who they were. That shit was turning me on. I went out into the front room to get another condom.

The nucca Eddie had two white bitches on the floor. He was hitting one from the back while she ate the other girl's pussy. I kneeled down over the girl who was getting her pussy ate, and tuck my dick in her mouth. She was holding my dick with one hand, guiding it against her tonsils and moving the head through the side of her jaw.

I grabbed another condom, then Eddie and I switched. Shawanna was right, them hoes were new. That lil' pink pussy felt like a silk glove, sliding back and forth on my dick. I couldn't stand another stroke. I pulled out and rolled the condom off. I was skeeting nut all in ole' girl's back and between the crack of her steaming ass, when Shawanna and Black stepped into the room.

Shawanna tried to act like she had an attitude because we had them white hoes in there. But I knew how to fix that. I made Shawanna get down on her knees, and licked my nut from between ole' girl's ass.

We thrashed them hoes all night…

Chapter Twenty-One

Back in Detroit, Eddie and Black cheesed like two little kids as we drove down John R in the back of Mile's limousine. They were looking out the window at the ghetto activity going on. We all laughed at the sight of an apparent crackhead busting out the front door of Imperial Grocery store. In his hands, he was carrying some frozen meat. He was running full speed with an old Arab man on his heels swinging a bat. That shit was hilarious.

We needed that laugh because it was probably gonna be the last time we smiled in a while. We had business to take care of. I picked up the car phone and called Mr. Davidson at his office.

"Any word yet?"

"I think they're using a different last name, but I have someone on top of it. Just give me some time, and in the meantime, do whatever you've been doing."

"What's that?" I asked.

"Keeping your nose clean. We have to let this heat die down a bit and I told you what I feared would happen. Well, it's happened."

"Give it to me."

"The FBI are working the case now. So, you have to be very careful. Corey, listen to me good."

"I'm listening."

"If you let them catch you before we're able to successfully complete operation snatch, I'm afraid that you will receive a life sentence. They pretty much have an open and shut case."

I hung up the phone. Mr. Davidson's words kept replaying in my head. A life sentence wasn't even in my language. I'd rather die in the streets like a legend, than to spend the rest of my life behind bars.

"What's wrong, Coach? You don't look too good, my nucca," said Black.

"The feds is on us," I said, before closing my eyes.

"You mean like the Federallies?" asked Eddie.

"Yeah. That be them," I said. I hadn't told Eddie and Black about the choke move downtown at the Renaissance Center and that's the real reason the FBI was getting involved.

"Who was that on the phone?" asked Black.

"Our lawyer, Mr. Davidson. He put me on some game that will save our asses, but it's a hit or miss deal. If we blow it, we might as well head for the border and never look back."

"Shit, what's good? What we gotta do? asked Eddie.

"Yeah. You know we down to do whatever and anything to get Nick out. And anything to keep us from going in, let's do it," said Black.

"He's 'pose to get back with me on some information, and then we can take it from there. In between now and then, we gotta stay low to the ground. If you must go out, have Miles send a limo to get you. All spots are shut down permanently."

"What you mean permanently?" asked Black.

"We're getting too much money now to be still that hands-on with the shit. All we dealing with is bricks. If a nucca ain't snatching fifty or better, we ain't fuckin' with em'. That way, we can eliminate having to deal with so many nuccas who may be potential slave catchers. For right now, Jose, Lex and Spoon are the only nucca's we serving."

"So, what we 'pose to do, sit back and twiddle our fuckin' thumbs all day?" asked Eddie.

"Nah, trust me, you got a full time job now that the feds are involved. It's called staying alive and free," I said.

We turned down Caldwell at the corner of 7 Mile. I looked Keith and Cane in their face from behind the tinted window of the limo, they were leaning against Cane's black El Darado, parked outside Sheeba's bar. The sight of them made my blood boil, 'cause I knew that their slimy asses had something to do with King David's death. They were Dump's flunkies, so I knew they were in on it. Just as soon as I could fix the Crew's situation, I was going to kill Keith and Cane...

We rode through the Zone, turning the heads of spectator's as the limo inched by. Despite our absence, the Zone was in full swing. Little kids were outside playing tag, which took me back to the days of when me, Black, Lil' Pimp, Rome, and Rocko were just jits.

It's funny how people change, I thought as we continued on crossing Stockton side street.

"Look at ole' Lester," laughed Black.

Lester was an old friend of King David's. He was also a crackhead, probably the first crackhead in the Zone. Lester had been smoking for as long as I can remember. Today was no different, he had a sofa strapped down to a shopping cart, pushing it back up toward 7 Mile. The few nuccas that remained, as far as hustlas, were hunched over on the corner of Hillsdale shooting two dice.

Nobody seemed to miss our presence. It was true, life goes on. I thought to myself that if we were to get knocked and go to jail, nuccas would still be doing them. Somebody else would step up and take our places, supplying the coke. And we'd be just a story the old heads would tell from time to time. I couldn't let the Crew go out like that.

As we rode pass my house on Caldwell, I could see that the privacy fence to the Pit-bull farm was leaning in. I sat up in my seat as we sat dead center of the house. The front door had a large board on it with a white sheet of paper attached to it. I couldn't make out all the words, but I could see the three taunting letters in big bold black ink.

"F.B.I.," read Eddie.

"Pull off," I instructed the driver. My insides were turning. All of a sudden I felt the need to shit. The feds had hit the crib. All the money we had, and yet our world seemed to be getting smaller by the day. That's what the feds do to you. They have the resources to make your world close in on you.

"Damn, my nucca. Them bitches ain't playing no games," said Black. His eyes were bucked, as he sat at the edge of his seat.

"That's what I've been tryna' tell you," I said.

We rode pass Black's detail shop, and it was the same thing. The feds had left Black a little note. They had left a note at his house on Healey too. The shit, I ain't gone lie, it was spooky. It felt like they were watching us just then, even with the tinted windows. I ordered the driver to leave the city. We crossed 8 Mile Road on Mound into Warren, Michigan. I told the driver to just drive. I picked up the car phone and dialed my house number. I crossed my fingers while the phone was ringing that the feds hadn't found that house, otherwise me, Black, and Eddie might be sleeping in the limo.

"Hello." Jackie answered on the seventh ring.

"Is everything alright, baby?" I asked.

"Corey? Where are you?"

"Yes, everything's fine. Why'd you say that?"

"I'm just checking on you. Has anyone been by the house?"

"No. Other than my mother, no."

"Has anybody called there looking for me?"

"No, Corey. Baby, is something wrong?" asked Jackie, sounding concerned.

I sat back at ease, then took a deep breath. "Nah, everything is going to be fine," I said.

"Where are you?"

"I'll see you in a minute. I love you." Click.

"What she say, they hit out there, too?" asked Eddie. He was nervously rolling a blunt.

"Nah. It seems to be the one place they didn't."

"Whose name is the house in?" asked Black.

"You know I had the old man up at Exotic Cars plug me. He did it through a broker," I said.

"That's why then. It ain't in yo' name, so we should be good," said Black.

"Yeah, I was watching this special on A&E about how the feds build cases on nuccas. You know I get high and be on my intelligent shit," laughed Eddie. He took a hit from his L, then continued.

"They were saying how the feds use what criminals give em'. It's like a puzzle. As criminals, we give them all the pieces and all they got to do to catch us is put them shits together. They was interviewing retired DEA agents and specialists. All of em' said the same thing. They were saying how they used paperwork to build cases and obtain convictions."

"What kind of paperwork?" asked Black.

"All types of paper trail; deeds to houses, bank accounts, receipts, pictures, handwritten notes, phone records, and statements made by rats. They put all that shit together and paint a vivid picture of who they want you to be in the eyes of a jury," said Eddie.

Listening to Eddie gave me the chills. I wondered what all the feds had taken out of the house on Caldwell…

Chapter Twenty-Two

"Get that fuckin' light outta my face," said Nick.
The deputy working the graveyard shift was standing in front of Nick's cell beaming his flash light in Nick's face. "What you wanna see some pink dick? You fuckin' faggot!" yelled Nick.
The deputy ran his keys across the iron bars of Nick's cell, making a loud clinking sound. He cut off his flash light and said, "Get dressed, you're leaving." The deputy turned and then disappeared down the dark hallway of the 9th floor.
"What the fuck he mean I'm leaving?" Nick rolled out of his wooden frame bunk, placing his bare feet on the cold concrete floor beneath him. Nick was still in 1300 Beaubien, Detroit Police headquarter's. His stay there had been nothing short of living in hell. The deputies hated his soul, because he was suspected of being involved in the murders of their fellow officers. They treated him like shit. And Nick had suspected that's exactly what they've been doing to his food, shitting in it. As a result, he only ate what the run-around brought him. Nick stood up and walked over to the bars and squinted, as he read the time on the clock hanging on the wall. It was 3:00 in the morning.

"That dick sucka playin' games," Nick climbed back in bed, but before he could situate the blanket over him, the deputy appeared at his cell with his flash light beaming in his face.

"Let's go. They're here to get you," said the deputy.

"Look, I don't know what type of games you playin' but I ain't feelin' this shit," said Nick.

"Young man, I am not playing any games. There are some people here to get you. Now get dressed and leave all that other stuff. I don't think you'll be coming back here."

Nick slid his socks on, then his shoes. He stepped to the sink, and splashed some water on his face, then raced to the cell bars. Nick was happy as E-mothafucka' to be leaving 1300, he didn't care where he was going, as long as it wasn't there. The deputy unlocked Nick's cell and slid the door open. Stepping into the hallway, Nick fell in step with the deputy as they round the corner and stepped onto the dilapidated elevator.

Down in registry, standing at the desk were two U.S. Marshal's dressed in blue khaki suits, bearing silver five point star badges on their shirts. The deputy handed Nick over to the Marshals who immediately began hooking belly chains and ankle bracelets on Nick.

"Who are ya'll?" asked Nick.

"Were with the United States Marshal Service," one of the men answered, as he clipped a pad lock onto the belly chain. "Where y'all taking me?" asked Nick.

The Marshals shut down all communication with Nick. They had identified themselves and that was all the information they were parting with. They signed the release of custody paperwork, then ushered Nick out the back of the building to an awaiting silver 15 passenger van with tinted windows.

From the back of the van, Nick looked out the window at the city. They were moving through downtown Detroit. The van stopped at a light on Gratiot in front of City Slicker's and Broadway's. Nick smiled to himself at the thought of him and the Crew copping some blocks and throwing that shit on. That split moment of happiness was short-lived, as the light turned green and the van pulled off bringing Nick back to reality.

The van made a sudden turn and ducked low into the ground tunnel of the court house on Lafayette Blvd. Nick turned around to see the metal sliding door shut. It was like the bat cave down there, he thought. The van stopped at a control booth. One of the Marshals said something to the man inside the booth, then cut off the engine. They pulled Nick from the van and escorted him up a ramp. The

Marshals had Nick by his belly chain, pushing him up the ramp making the ankle bracelets cut into his skin.

"Can we slow down? These fuckin' cuffs are killing me," said Nick.

The Marshals were like robots. They had no compassion. They continued pusing Nick to the top of the ramp where the elevator sat. They stepped off the elevator on the 11th floor, and led Nick to the office of U.S. Assistant attorney Robert Lech. Inside the office sat four bodies, they all rose to their feet as Nick entered the room.

"Thank you," one of the men sitting close to the door said, talking to the Marshals.

"Please, have a seat, Nick," the man said pulling the chair he had been sitting in to the center of the floor.

Nick took a seat reluctantly. He was shaking like a crap game, but he knew the score. No matter what, keep ya' mouth shut until your lawyer showed up.

"How are you, Nick? You don't mind if I call you Nick do ya'? Of how about White boy Nick?" asked the man who had given Nick his chair.

"Listen, Nick, we're here to help you," another man beside Nick said.

"Do you know why you're here?" asked the man seated behind the desk. Nick didn't answer. "Your case has been turned over to the F.B.I. and I am the U.S. Attorney assigned to your case. My name is Robert Lech. And these fine men here are the agents assigned to your case. They're with the Federal Bureau of Investigation."

All the agents introduced themselves to Nick.

"Now that we're all acquainted, let's get to the reason of this meeting. Nicky boy, you're in a lot of shit. But the good thing is that you're the first one to get caught. You have the opportunity to seek the best possible deal, that is if your willing to help yourself. Are you willing to help yourself, Nick?" asked the U.S. Attorney Lech.

Nick just stared Mr. Lech in the face, not saying a word.

"Maybe I should explain to you what charges you're facing; you're going to be charged with aiding and abetting, two counts of murder for the police homicides, carrying a concealed weapon and continuing a criminal enterprise..."

Nick face tightened, as Mr. Lech noticed. Him along with all the agents standing in the room were trained to read body language. Mr. Lech leaned over Nick, getting up close and personal. "What, you didn't think we knew you all were trafficking drugs? We know everything about you, Nicky boy," said Lech.

Nick cleared his throat of the nervous lump which had been trying to set in since he got off the elevator. Looking Mr.

Lech square in his face, Nick stated. "Since you know everything about me, you should know that I'm not a rat. And I want my lawyer."

"You're making a huge mistake, Nick," one of the agents said.

Another agent chimed in, "Yeah, Nick, once the grand jury indicts you, it's outta our hands. I mean you'd still be able to offer cooperation and possibly receive lesser time, but what we're offering you here is complete immunity. Right now is your chance to save yourself. We can put you into the Witsec program, whatever it takes to get you on board. If you decide to help us, you won't even be indicted. We can say that you are an informant assisting us in the investigation of others."

"It's your only chance," said Lech.

"I'd rather take my chances with twelve," said Nick.

"Twelve what?" asked Lech.

"Twelve jurors," laughed Nick.

Mr. Lech's jaws tightened. "Get him out of here and tell the Marshals to put him on Diesel Therapy until further notice," ordered Lech.

"What the fuck is diesel therapy?" asked Nick.

The agents all laughed. They snatched Nick from his chair, then hustled him out of the office. The agents handed Nick off to the Marshals in the hallway and gave them Lech's orders.

The Marshals escorted Nick onto the elevator, getting off in the bat cave. They packed Nick into the back of the van and came from under the tunnel like a bat out of hell, making a screeching right turn into the wee hour traffic.

They had been driving for hours. They were in some rural area Nick never knew existed. He kept firing questions at the Marhals, to none of which were answered. Finally, the Marshal behind the wheel got tired of hearing Nick's voice, so he cranked the radio full blasts. The passenger turned and looked at Nick and yelled over the music.

"What? I can't hear you," he was laughing in Nick's face. Between them was a metal gate. Nick felt like a K-9 inside of a dog kennel. The farther they drove, the more paranoid Nick became. He was beginning to think that they were going to take him somewhere and kill him, and burn his body with diesel fuel. That was the only thing he could come up with from Lech's diesel therapy. The van made an unsuspected turn onto a dirt road through a wooded area. If the average person was traveling the road, he wouldn't even have seen the small passage.

'Yeah, they're about to stank me,' Nick thought as the van pulled onto a small patch of land coming to a complete stop. They were no longer in the woods. The van was parked at the edge of the trail on-looking the patch of land ahead. Nick was about to shit on himself because the fright was so intense. They were just sitting listening to hard-rock for hours. At the start of the land, the nose of a small plane could be seen as it landed. The plane came to a halt, stopping just yards short of the van. The Marshal behind the wheel turned down the radio. Leaning forward with his eyes on the plane, he asked his partner. "Is that your guy?"

"Sure is," answered the second Marshal. "I'll be right back," he said climbing out the van.

Nick watched the Marshal like a hawk as he said something to the pilot. The Marshal waved his partner over.

"Show time," said the driver. He got out and walked around to the side of the van, opening Nick's door as he held his hand out.

"Come on, they're waiting," said the Marshal.

"Who's waiting?" asked Nick.

"The air crew, now come on, let's go."

"I'm not getting on no fuckin' plane."

"We can do this the easy way or the hard way, but one way or another, you're going."
Nick didn't budge. The Marshal waved his partner over to the van. "What's going on?"
"This dick is refusing to get out of the van."
"We don't have time for this shit. Zap his ass and let's go."
"I'm giving you a direct order to step out of the van," said the Marshal, while pointing his tazer gun straight at Nick.
"I'm not... Ahh..." Nick shook like someone having a seizure.
The Marshal tasered his ass, and was lying on the trigger. When they finally let up off the juice, Nick laid slump over the seat bench with two coil cables stuck in his chest. He was slobbing out of the mouth and in a state of delirium. The two Marshals snatched Nick from the van and carried him onto the plane.
"If you as much as flinch, you're gonna ride the juice again," an air Marshal told Nick, as he fastened Nick's seatbelt. The cables were still in Nick's chest. All the Marshal had to do was squeeze the trigger and Nick would fry.

The two Marshals that drove Nick on the van stepped off the plane; they shut the exit, then tapped the plane for takeoff. Within seconds the plane was up in the air. Nick was drained from the zap. He fought to keep his eyes open, but the drowsiness got the best of him. He closed his eyes, falling into a deep sleep.

*****

Bang! Bang! Bang! Nick sat up in this bunk to see a female guard standing at his cell door. Bang! Bang! Bang! She banged on the door with her keys. "Breakfast," she said.

Nick rolled out of the bed and went to the door to get the Styrofoam tray inside the food slot and the milk carton beside it. The woman shut the slot and was about to walk away.

"Excuse me," Nick called the woman back. "Can you tell me where I'm at? I don't remember getting here."

"You're in Keewenaw County," said the guard.

"Kewa what?" asked Nick.

"You're up north. You know the Upper Peninsula, the U.P," the woman tried explaining.

From her accent, Nick could tell that wherever he was, it wasn't any where close to home.

The guard continued to fill Nick in. "Yeah, they flew you in yesterday. You slept most of the night away. They say they had to taser you to get you on the plane. You're on diesel therapy."

"What's that?"

"Here today, gone tomorrow. You might wanna get some rest, you'll be leaving in the early morning."

"Where am I going? " asked Nick.

"Beats me. That's why they call it diesel therapy. You'll figure it out," the guard said, then walked away.

Chapter Twenty-Three

"Corey, is everything alright?"

"Why you ask that?"

"I called and talked to Ms. Davis, you know my old friend who owns Sheeba's? She told me that she rode pass my house and the doors were all boarded up. What's going on Corey? And don't you lie to your mother," said Tina.

"Some things happened but nothing that I can't fix," I said.

"Do I need to get on a plane and come home? Cause you know I will."

"Calm down, Ma. I can handle it. You just focus on your treatment and getting ya' self back in order. Everything will still be standing when you get back," I assured Tina.

"Alright then. You know I'm still your momma, and I'm gonna worry. You make sure you stay clear of trouble. I'll be finished with my treatment in two weeks. I know, I can expect to see you front and center at my graduation" asked Tina.

She was still out in Cali, getting herself together. "I wouldn't miss it for nothing in the world."

Well, alright I'ma let you go. I gotta get ready for my evening class. I'm giving a testimony of my life. Cross ya' fingers for me, and know how I get nervous speaking in front of lots of people.

"I will. I love you, Ma."

"Ah, I love you too, Corey. You take care now." Click…

"Ahh… That's so sweet. My baby's a momma's boy," said Jackie, as she leaned over and kissed me on the side of my face.

It was Saturday morning, and we were playing husband and wife, laid up in our PJ's.

"I thought you said you were going to tell her about me the next time you talked to her," said Jackie sitting up in bed.

"Baby, you heard what we were talking about. It totally didn't cross my mind. I was just hoping she hadn't heard about me being all over the News."

"I understand, how is she?" asked Jackie.

"She sounds good. In two weeks, she'll be finished with her treatment and will graduate. I promised her I'd be there. I'm taking you with me, so you can meet her then."

"You're the best," said Jackie, kissing me again.

"Now I need you to do a lil' something for me," I said softly, while looking deep into Jackie's eyes.

"And what might that be?" asked Jackie.

"I need for you to knock some of this stress up off me."

"Where is it? Show me," said Jackie in the voice tone of a nurse.

I grabbed jackie's hand and rubbed it down my chest, stopping at my dick. "You feel that?" I asked.

"Yeah," answered Jackie. "It feels like its throbbing. Definitely a lot of swelling," she said stroking my dick as if she were examining it.

"You think you can get the swelling to go down?"

"That shouldn't be a problem," said Jackie as she inhaled the head of my dick.

"Ahh. That's it, right there… Ahh…" I leaned back against the plush pillows and closed my eyes, while Jackie took the stress away…

About five minutes into it, my moment of paradise was interrupted by the ringing of the phone. I opened my eyes, knowing I had to take the call. Only four people had my home number and each of their calls were deemed important. "Don't stop, baby," I said reaching for the phone on the nightstand. "Who this?"

"Corey, it's me, Mr. Davidson."

"What's up Mr. D. Give me some news I can use."

"Well, here's some news but I don't know if you can use it. As I told you, the feds have picked up your investigation. It seems that they've moved Nick early this morning."

"Moved him where?"

"That's the funny thing about it, I have not the slightest idea. I called a few contacts of mine and they informed me that the U.S. Attorney assigned to the case put him on diesel therapy."

"What the hell is diesel therapy?"

"That's when they bounce you around from jail to jail by plane, bus, car, mule, or any other means of transfer. The feds are dirty players, so do yourself a favor and don't expect a fair fight 'cause it ain't happening. Nick could be anywhere right now. And tomorrow he'll be somewhere else. And the same thing goes for the next day. They do that shit for two reasons. One, so your mail and lawyer correspondence won't ever reach you. And two, so hopefully you'll break weak. I must tell you that a lot people do fall weak. That's why they call it diesel therapy."

"What do you mean by falling weak?"

"Rolling over, snitching, ratting whatever you wanna call it."

"We don't have to worry about that with Nick, he's a rida," I said confidently.

"Corey, let me tell you something and I want you to listen good. You're in the big now, you can't put anything past anyone. No one around you is above suspicion…"

"What about the other thing. You got any insight for me on that?"

"Yes. Grab a pen."

I pulled Jackie up from my dick, as I looked for a pen. "Go ahead," I said.

"Julian Mackie and Tavon Townsend."

"Townsend?" I repeated. "You sure on that second one?" I asked.

"Yeah, I double checked them both. I trust that this will all be a thing of the past soon?"

"Withoug a doubt but uh, what's the name of the school?"

"I'm sorry, you know I'm getting old. It's called Fredrick Douglass School of Performing Arts, it's on…"

"I know where it is. Thank you Mr. D."

"A'ight, you give me a holler when everything's situated and as for the pines, the wife loved it," said Mr. Davidson.

I laughed. "A'ight. Talk to you soon." Click.

Jackie tried to finish what she started, but I refused her. I was sick about the news regarding Nick. How was I supposed to be laid up getting dome, while my man was on some mental torture expedition? I took a deep breath, then rolled out of bed.

"Where are you going?" asked Jackie.

"I've gotta take care of something," I said, putting on my clothes. "Do me a favor and call Miles and tell em' to send me a limo," I said, heading into the bathroom.

I looked in the mirror after washing my face. "Why did you give that bastard my last name?" I asked, as if Amanda were standing before me.

Chapter Twenty-Four

Back at the U.S. Attorney's office.

"Boss, I think we may have a break in the Crew's case," F.B.I. special agent Dale Hous, informed U.S. Attorney, Robert Lech.

Lech leaped from his seat and raced to close the door behind agent Hous. "Have a seat," Lech, pulled Hous a chair out from in front of his desk. Sitting on the edge of the desk, Lech quizzed. "So, tell me this break you have."

"This morning DEA conducted a control buy from a guy they'd been investigating for a while. I don't know if Steven Jackson rings any bells? They call him Spoon on the streets."

"Not familiar with the name, but please finish."

"Well, DEA purchased two kilo grams of crack cocaine from Mr. Spoon, using an informant. Spoon, is downstairs in the holding cell wishing to speak with you. He says that the coke belongs to our guy Coach."

Lech could barely contain himself, as he raced around his desk and dialed the Marshal's extension. "Yes, please have someone bring, what's his name…?"

"Steven Jackson," said agent Hous.

"Yes, have someone bring Steven Jackson, up to my office right away. This is Lech."
Within minutes, two Marshals were ushering Spoon off the elevator and into Lech's office.
"Please have a seat, what is it, Spoon?" asked Lech, as he pulled out a chair.
"Marshal, can you please be sure to order us some Chinese food. I think we're going to be here for quite a while. Go ahead and give the Marshal your order, Spoon," Lech said. He was rolling out the red carpet to hell, in hopes that Spoon would sell his soul to the devil and roll over on Coach. After the Marshal took their orders, Lech had them remove all of Spoon's restraints.
"Now, isn't that much better?" asked Lech.
"Yeah, much better," said Spoon.
"Okay, so tell me what happened? Agent Hous here says you sold some coke to an informant this morning," said Lech.
"Yeah…" said Spoon.
"It's not that bad. It's not like you killed anyone. Agent Hous also tells me that you wanted to speak with me regarding how you came to possess the coke in the first place. Let me start by saying that I think you're doing what's in your best interest by helping yourself. If you help

me, I can assure you that you will be helped in return. Is that something you'd be interested in?" asked Lech.

"Yeah," said Spoon.

"Alright. Then start by telling me who you got the coke from, and when?"

"I got the coke from Eddie. He gave it to me 'bout a week ago.

"You mean this man?" asked Lech, handing Spoon a picture.

"Yeah," Spoon confirmed that was Eddie in the picture.

"Can you tell me the names of these other men?" Lech handed Spoon three more pictures.

"Yeah, this is Nick right here, that's Black, and that's Coach," Spoon identified all the men in the pictures correctly.

Lech was screaming for joy on the inside because he knew that Spoon wasn't lying. He was their man!

"Okay, so tell me how you know these men," said Lech.

"I met Coach a while back at an event. We exchanged info, and he stopped by my house one day outta the blue and dropped two keys on me. We've been doin' business ever since," said Spoon.

"But you said that you got the two kilos the DEA bought you from Eddie."

"Coach, has been having me deal with Eddie lately. You know Coach is the boss of the Crew. He just calls the shots," said Spoon.

"I see. So, when was the last time you scored some coke from Eddie, and when can you score again?" asked Lech.

"I ain't got nothin' from Eddie in 'bout a week. I can get something whenever I need it. All I gotta do is call em' and he'll bring it right over," said Spoon.

"Are you willing to make a controlled buy? You know, just how the situation went down with you this morning," said Lech.

"If it'll help me, yeah but I owe him for the two keys ya'll took."

"Don't worry about that. I'll take care of it. Agent Hous will set it up and make sure everything is settled," said Lech.

Chapter Twenty-Five

"They got this bitch surrounded like she's the first lady or something," Eddie was talking about Amanda. She had pulled up in a four car caravan, and was let out at the curb with her two boys.

"I say we just slaughter all their asses, right fuckin' now," said Black, passing me the L. We were parked outside Fredrick Douglas School, across the street in the back of the limo. The fed thought they were watching us, but we were watching them.

Agents sat parked in their cars while Amanda and her two boys entered the school. Everything so far had happened just the way Hank said it would. Hank was a private investigator that Mr. Davidson turned me onto. He had been watching the school inside and out and relayed his findings to me. Hank told him that every morning like clockwork at 7:50, the caravan pulls up to the school. Amanda gets out and personally escorts the two boys inside the school. She sees them to their classes, and then returns to the awaiting caravan, which then leaves with one car and two men staying back to watch the boys in their classes.

We watched as Amanda exited the school, she climbed into the back seat of a tinted out Crown Victoria, then three of the four cars pulled away, leaving one car behind.

"Tomorrow, we hit. Driver, let's go," I said.

"So, how we gonna get the boys outta there?" asked Eddie. Didn't you say that it's two agents in there with em'?

"I'm not saying the shit is going to be easy. It's going to have to go down just how we plan, or we can blow the entire move," I said.

"I'm listening," said Eddie.

"Here's what we gonna do. The whole objective is to get this bitch to leave the witness protection voluntarily. Since they're not going to just let her walk away without following her everywhere she goes, she's gonna have to sneak away."

"And why would she do that, when she knows we're tryna' kill her ass?" asked Black.

"She'll do it in hopes of saving her boys. The P.I. told me that the reason she doesn't let the agents escort the boys in or pick them up is because Amanda doesn't want the other kids picking on them. Every day after school, Amanda goes to the office and waits for the bell to ring. When she comes in the office tomorrow, she will be handed the phone and given instructions…"

"That shit sounds official," said Eddie smiling.

"Yeah, but you still didn't say how we were going to get the boys," said Black.

"The same way we're gonna get Amanda, through the phone. The agents will be sitting in the back of the classroom. None of the kids nor the teacher know who they are or why they're there. When the agent hears his name over the intercom to report to the office, he'll get up and go to the office. However, he'll never make it because you are going to be in the mop closet. We'll wait twenty minutes, and then page the other one. Same thing, we're going to have to be on the same page, though. We gotta get this done in a small window of time. We don't need any surprises," I said.

"Yeah, that shit's official, my nucca. I gotta give it to you," said Black, hitting rocks with me.

Beep! Beep! Beep! Eddie's pager went off. "This that nucca Spoon, he put the code in, so he must be out. Have the driver take me up to Miles, so I can snatch a limo," said Eddie.

"How's business?" I asked.

"You know, no matter what, nuccas is gone always shop," said Black.

"Like now," said Eddie.

"A'ight. Ya'll just be careful out here cause it's a lot of people who want us out the way right now. And I'm not just talkin' 'bout the feds..."

*****

We dropped Eddie off at Miles, so he could get a limo.

"If you need me, I'll be at the crib," I said, then hit rocks with Eddie.

I dropped Black off at one of his chick's crib, then had the driver take me home.

Chapter Twenty-Six

"Listen up," Agent Hous clapped his hands loudly. Everyone stopped what they were doing to focus in on what Hous was about to say. He was standing dead center of Spoon's living room, where he and a host of other federal agents set up shop. "We've just made contact with our guy. He is said to be on his way now, at which time we will administer a controlled buy. I need everyone to take their positions, and hold them until I give the cue to take em' down. Alright, let's go," Agent Hous clapped his hands once more, and the pack dispersed…

Spoon was pacing the living room floor with his head down, while mumbling something to himself. "Spoon, get over here, so we can hook you up." Agent Hous was holding a thin wire in his hand that had tape on both ends. Spoon looked up in a frantic state.

"I don't know if I can do this," said Spoon, as he went back to pacing the floor, mumbling… Agent Hous rushed over and grabbed Spoon by the arm, spinning him around. He looked Spoon dead in the eyes, then said. "Oh, you're going to do it or you're gonna do hard prison time. You need to pull your shit together and put this fucking wire on!" yelled Hous. He slammed the wire into Spoon's chest and held it there until Spoon took it. All that royal treatment shit they had shown Spoon over at the U.S. Attorney's office was over. He was now a bonified registered rat and would be treated as such.

Spoon looked at the wire in his hand. 'This is what I've become' he thought. Reluctantly, he raised his shirt over his head, while Agent Hous strapped the wire to his chest.

Ring! Ring! Ring! The phone sitting on the stand beside the sofa lit up. "Answer it," Hous handed Spoon the phone.

"Answer it, damn it!" yelled Hous.

"What up, doe?" answered Spoon.

The special agent seated at the living room table pushed play on the machine before him, and two reel wheels begin spinning, recording the conversation.

"I'm turning down yo' block now, be outside," Eddie said hanging up the car phone in the back of his limo.

Agent Hous radioed his team. "Our man is on his way. Hold your position. I repeat, hold your positions." Here, and don't let me down," said Hous. He stuffed a book bag into Spoon's chest…

"Hit the horn at this next house," said Eddie. He was giving orders to the pretty new driver. She was a half breed yellow bone. Eddie had seen her at the service center, and requested that she drove him. He'd been flirting with her since they pulled away from Mile's limousine service. Everytime she'd close the divider. Eddie would roll it back down and say something slick to her. Eventually, she got tired of rolling the divider up so she left it down.

Bom! Bom!

"Our guy is in that limo," advised Hous across the radio.

"Roger."

Spoon came out the house, and looked up and down the block while walking to the back of the limo.

Eddie popped the locks for Spoon, then slid over to the next seat.

"What up, doe?" asked Eddie, as Spoon shut the door.

"Ain't shit. What's good?" Spoon gave Eddie dap.

"Damn, nucca. Why yo' hand so wet?" asked Eddie, wiping his hand on the seat.

"I was in there cookin' up the last of the shit I had left," said Spoon.

"A'ight. So, what you got for me?" asked Eddie.

"This is um. Huh, five hun'd stacks," mumbled Spoon, he was fiddling with the zipper on the book bag, while leaning over.

Looking down Spoon's shirt, Eddie's eyes lit up at the sight of the wire. He looked up and scanned the block but didn't see anything unusual. "I can't get this damn thing to open," Spoon said. He was still wrestling with the zipper.

Eddie reached over and turned up the radio full blast. He slid to the front of the limo and told the driver to pull off. Spoon looked up as the limo started moving. He was staring down the barrel of Eddie's 50 cal. Desert Eagle.

"The limo is moving, what do you want us to do, boss? Asked one of the field agent.

Agent Hous was trying to make a decision.

"What do you want us to do, boss? The limo is almost at the end of the street. Over!"

"I can't hear anything, except loud music," said the technician working the recorder.

"That son of a bitch tipped him off!" yelled Hous. "This is Hous. Take em' down. I repeat, take em' down!"

Boom! Boom! Boom! Eddie shot Spoon in the head three times, splattering brains all over the rear window. Before Spoon's body hit the floor, Eddie was pushing him out the limo. Out of nowhere, white men filled the block on both sides of the street. They were inching towards the limo with their guns drawn. The driver slammed on the brakes bringing the limo to a complete stop.

"Bitch, pull off!" yelled Eddie.

The woman was screaming at the top of her lungs and trembling. She had seen Eddie blow Spoon's top off. Eddie didn't care what she was going through, and the fact that she was fine all that shit was out the window.

Two Chevy Lumina's bent the corner and was heading in the direction of the limo. Eddie sprung into action. He grabbed the driver by the neck and pulled her body through the divider. He put his gun to her head and pulled the trigger. Boom! One lone shot knocked a patch out the top of ole' girl's dome.

Eddie climbed through the divider behind the wheel and slapped the limo into drive. The tires screeched as the limo bit down and sped off. The agent who had been standing with their guns drawn opened fired on the limo as it sped off… Boom! Boom!... Shots riddled the limo. Eddie was ducked low, steering the wheel with one hand. "Ahh!" he yelled, as a bullet ripped through the driver's door and into his thigh.

Eddie sat up and stared the Lumina dead in its face. He pushed down on the gas even harder…

"This fucker is crazy," said the agent behind the wheel of the Lumina. The agent swerved to the right just in time missing the limo only by inches. The second Lumina

wasn't so lucky, Eddie side swiped the passenger side doing every bit of 80 mph. The Lumina did a 360° spin and smacked a parked car at the curb.
"Do not let him get away!" yelled Hous over his radio. "Fuck!" Hous threw his radio against the wall breaking it. He and the technician bolted for the door. They jumped into Hous's Tahoe, and joined the chase…
Eddie turned onto Joy Rd. doing 60 mph, making the limo fish tail into passing traffic. He banked the side of a Detroit police cruiser with the ass of the limo, caught the wheel and hit the gas. The cruiser threw on its lights, and joined the chase. Hrrrrr… Eddie hit a hard left turn nearly hitting a woman crossing the street. He opened the limo up top speed, as he sped down the ramp leading onto the Southfield Expressway. Honnn! The horn of an eighteen-wheeler sounded at the sight of the limo exiting the ramp. The eighteen-wheeler slammed on its brakes to avoid collision with the limo. It jack-knifed, and flipped over the medium causing a massive pile up.

Despite Eddie's reckless driving, the feds and Detroit police were on the limo's bumper. Eddie looked in the rear-view mirror through the back window which was shattered. He was blinded by the glaring red and blue lights. He continued to floor the limo down the expressway, purposely driving like a mad man. He started side swiping every car and truck he passed. He was hoping that they'd see the way he was driving, and would call the chase off. But Hous was determined not to let Eddie get away. Eddie started looking for an out. But every exit he approached, at the top of the ramp sat a police cruiser with its lights on.

The freeway had to end and Eddie knew it. He looked over to his right, and above he could see the Channel 4 News ghetto bird was on him. "Damn," said Eddie as if to accept his fate. He looked in the mirror trying to come to grips with reality. "Fuck it," he said reaching in his pocket pulling out a sack of Gan's and a half broken Swiser blunt. Driving with one hand, Eddie put the limo on cruise control, while he rolled what he knew would be his last blunt. "I'ma die high," said Eddie lighting the L. He took a long pull, then reached over and grabbed the car phone between the console.

"What up, doe?" said Eddie, exhaling smoke through his nose.

"Ain't shit. Chilling with wifey. What's good my nucca, where you at?" I asked.

"Turn the News on," said Eddie.

I was sitting behind my desk inside the pool house. Eddie's call had interrupted my thoughts, I was thinking about tomorrow. The day when I'd burry Amanda's funky ass once and for all.

"I'm looking, but I don't see nothing," I said, flipping through the channels.

"Turn it to Channel 4," said Eddie.

I flicked the remote to Channel 4. At the top of the screen read: Breaking News… there was an aerial view from a helicopter, it was following a black Lincoln limo, with police in tow.

"What happed, how'd they get on you?" I asked.

"Fuckin' faggot, Spoon tried to set me up."

"What?"

"When I went to serve him, he was actin' all 'noid and shit. I peeped game that the nucca was wearing a wire, so I stanked his ass."

"So, where are you going?" I asked. I felt helpless.

"To hell, if I don't pray. One thing's for certain, I'm not going back to jail."

"Damn, my nucca…" I was thinking of something to say, but no words seemed to fit.

"I just called to holla' at you one last time, my nucca," said Eddie, swerving out of the way of a spike strip a sherrif slid onto the road. Eddie had crossed 8 Mile, heading into the suburbs. The further he drove, the more counties joined the chase.

"Pull over E. I'll get you the best lawyer's money can buy," I said. I didn't want to see Eddie go out like this. We had come too far…

"Coach, I'm not going to prison for the rest of my life. I'd rather die right here, than to go back."

"E, man do it for me. I need you dawg."

"I love you too my nucca. I can honestly say this though, it's been real. I had my run, but now it's over. You take care of the Crew…." Eddie dropped the phone.

There was a road block set up about a half mile away.

"Eddie. Eddie!" I yelled.

Eddie swerved over to the shoulder and tried in one last desperate attempt to escape, he gunned the limo up the grass hill, but its length and transmission caused the limo to stall out, and then roll backward. Eddie grabbed the door handle and rolled out of the limo gun in hand.

He ran to the top of the hill and stopped at the fence. Police were on the other side of the fence with their guns drawn.

"Get down!" An officer ordered Eddie.

Eddie turned around to see police climbing the hill behind him.

"Get down!" ordered the officer.

Eddie put the cold steel barrel of his 50 cal. to the side of his head, then pulled the trigger. Boom!

I could see Eddie's body slump to the ground, and police still inchig toward his lifeless body.

"What a tragegy..." The News anchor reported. "The suspect, Eddie Dillon, has just committed suicide, after a 45 minute chase with police. Again, Eddie Dillon, one fourth of the infamous Crew, has just ended his life by turning his own gun on himself. What a tragedy..."

I was in tears. My nucca had just killed himself live on TV. This wasn't how it was supposed to end. Eddie was Crew. He was family. I broke down to my knees and cried my soul out...

Chapter Twenty-Seven

In the past two days, Nick had been shipped to five different jails, in three different States. Each morning he had to go through the guessing game to find out where he was. The shit was starting to take its toll on Nick. The affects of diesel therapy had Nick on the ropes. Looking in the stainless steel polished mirror mounted on his cell wall, Nick told himself. "Fuck this shit, I'm going home."

He banged on the door using the steel coffee cup the guard had given him. Within seconds, a guard appeared at Nick's cell. "You betta stop all that damn fussin' for we's come in there and tie your ass down," said the guard. He had a country accent and was chewing tobacco.

"Where am I?" asked Nick.

"That depends," said the guard.

"Depends on what?" asked Nick.

"On how good you are at guessin', boy."

"Com on, not again with this shit. Can you please just tell me where I am?" pleaded Nick.

"What, you don't like the guessin' game? I'm guessin' your 'bout ready to break," said the guard. He had seen his share of diesel therapy victims, and through his experience he could tell when the vic was falling weak.

“I need to use the phone,” said Nick.

“That depends,” said the guard.

“Depends on what? Why does everything depend on something? Just bring me the phone!” snapped Nick.

“That depends,” said the guard, in a smart-aleck tone of voice.

“Argh!” screamed Nick. “Depends on what?” asked Nick. He was pulling at his hair.

“On who you’re calling. Who are you calling?”

“I’m calling my lawyer.”

“Hmm. Wrong answer. Is there anyone else you’d like to call?” asked the guard.

“My father.”

“Hmm. Wrong answer. That’s two strikes, one more and you’re out. Now, is there anyone else you’d like to call?”

The shit was like mental torture. The guard was waiting on Nick to ask the right question.

“I wanna contact U.S. Attorney, Robert Lech,” said Nick.

“Ding! Ding! Ding! And the winner is,” said the guard. “I’ll be right back with the phone. The guard pulled a phone on wheels to Nick’s cell and opened the foot slot, so Nick could use it. The guard dialed out then handed Nick the receiver through the food slot.

"Robert Lech, how may I help you?"

"Mr. Lech, it's me, Nick.

Lech sat up in his seat. "Nick, how's it going? You enjoying your travels?" asked Lech.

"Very fuckin' funny," said Nick.

"Where are you today?" asked Lech.

"Your guess is as good as mine. When is this shit going to stop?"

"That depends," said Lech, sounding like the guard. They were all on the same accord. Nick leaned his head back and closed his eyes. Shaking his head, he began to speak. "Depends on what?"

"It all depends on you, Nick. How bad do you wanna come home?"

"I'm listening," said Nick.

"You know what I want, Nicky boy. Let's not kid ourselves. You called me for what, to say hi?"

"Nah, I called because I was hoping we could sit down and talk, maybe reach some common ground."

"Nick, the only common ground I'm after is putting Coach and Black behind bars where they belong. By the way,

Eddie killed himself after a 45 minute chase on the highway with police."

"What?" asked Nick.

"This thing is getting very serious. You don't want to be left holding the short end of the stick when this all plays out, 'cause we're going to get Coach and Black one way or another. So, tell me Nick, shall I have them bring you home?" asked Lech.

"Yeah."

"And we're clear on our terms, are we not?"

"Yeah, we're clear," said Nick, blowing out air of frustrations.

"I swear to God, Nick. If you try and fuck me, or play any cat and mouse games, your ass will be on diesel therapy for two years."

"I got it," said Nick.

"Alright, I'll see you in my office first thing in the morning." Click.

Nick hung the phone up and went to lie down on his bunk. Eyes staring up at the ceiling, he tried to rationalize his decision. 'In twenty years, no one would even remember his name, or what happened for that matter. All he could think about was being back in Cali with his dad.

"Fuck that white boy Nick, bullshit," he said, then closed his eyes…

Chapter Twenty-Eight

The next morning, Nick was picked up by two Marshals from Jackson County Jail in Rhode Island. Nick had never thought in his life that he'd be so happy to see the police. He was cheesing from ear to ear as the Marshal's drove him to a private airport. This time they didn't have to taser him to get on the plane. Nick put one foot in front of the other, not even feeling the cold steel of the ankle cuffs, as it cut into his shins. He took his seat on the plane next to the window and smiled. "Home sweet home, here I come," he said.

The airplane touched down at the Metropolitan Airport in Romulus, Michigan. An awaiting van containing two Marshals, the same two who had tasered Nick days before, greeted him on the tarmac.

"Have a nice tour?" one of the Marshals laughed. They packed Nick into the van and sped off.

They were in the city within twenty minutes, and disappeared down into the bat cave.

"Thank you," said Lech. He was waiting on the ground floor when the Marshals escorted Nick up the ramp. "I can take it from here," said Lech. Together, he and Nick rode the elevator up to Lech's office, where he had agent Hous remove the cuffs from Nick.

"Nicky, boy. You look like you've got a tan," laughed Hous, as he removed Nick's restraints.

"Everybody's a fuckin' comedian round here, huh?"

"Have a seat, Nick. You hungry? Hold on," Lech picked up his desk phone and told the Marshals to bring up some pizza. Hanging up the phone, Lech jumped straight into it. "Let's not waste anytime. I want all the details. We'll start with how you met Coach and Black," said Lech. He was ready with a pen and pad in his hand.

"I met Coach while we were in middle school. He moved out to Fresno, where I was staying with my father. We met at school, but he didn't stay long. He went back home and I didn't see shim for like six years. Then out of nowhere, he shows up at my doorstep. He offered me a position and I took it."

"Position, what are you talking about? Be more specific," said Lech.

"With the Crew. Coach wanted me to help him with his drug operation back in Detroit."

"Where is Coach scoring from, who is he getting the coke from? I need names," said Lech.

Nick dropped his head. He didn't want to involve his father and get him into any trouble.

"Listen, Nick. Just so I make myself very clear. The condition of you helping yourself is based solely on you helping us. I don't want no half-ass information. It's all or nothing here. Now if you know, tell me. Who is Coach getting the coke from?" asked Lech.

"If I tell you, will this information be used in anyway against that person?" asked Nick.

"Well, eventually of course it will," said Lech.

"See the thing is, it's a family member. And I can't see myself crossing those waters," said Nick.

"It will all come to light when we catch Coach. Do you honestly think he's going to keep your family members identity safe? No, he'll use it as a bargaining chip. But if you help me, I can see to it that a great portion of your assistance goes toward your family member's situation. Sorta like a package deal,"

After thinking for a moment, Nick took a deep breath, then exhaled. "He's getting it from my dad," said Nick.

"And what's your dad's name?" Lech scribbled something onto his notepad, then waited for Nick to give him a name.

"Nick, but they call em', Torch…" said Nick.

Agent Hous' face lit up like he'd hit the lotto. "Excuse me, Lech can I speak to you in the hallway for just a moment," said Hous. He and Lech excused themselves into the hall, Lech shutting the door behind them. "What's going on?" asked Lech.

Agent Hous, grabbed Lech by both arms, and began whispering. He could hardly conceal his excitement. "Do you know who Torch is?" asked Hous.

"No, who is he?" asked Lech.

"Hells Angles, Torch. One of the seated board members of the infamous motorcycle gang based out in California, and has been spreading their wings across the nation. We've been investigating the Angles forever, but nothing's ever been able to stick. If this is the same Torch, which I'm almost certain it is, then this thing is bigger than lil' Coach and the Crew. We're talking about international crimes being committed, here," said Hous.

"Okay, assuming that it is our guy, Torch. What do you suggest we do?" asked Lech.

"If Nick's willing to fully cooperate, and of course, with your approval, I suggest that we hold off on bringing the Crew down, as part of an ongoing investigation.

"You mean like, a superseding indictment?"

"Exactly. Through Nick, we'll be able to connect the dots to all kind of criminal enterprises. Some that we may not even know exist…"

"Let's do it," said Lech.

Chapter Twenty-Nine

I couldn't even look Black in his eyes, as he stepped through the front door of my house. He hugged Jackie, then I followed Black out back to the pool area. We sat across from one another at the table under the big patio umbrella. We still hadn't said one word to each other, nor did we make eye contact. Black broke into tears. I had never seen him like this. Out of all my years of knowing Black, I had never seen him cry. I didn't even know that he could. As hard as life had been on Black, one would think he was immune to pain.

Growing up watching both his parents strung out on crack was Black's turmoil. Eddie was Crew, part of our family. Losing him made Black and me both want to throw in the towel. Seeing Black breakdown like that brought tears to my eyes, but this time my tears weren't for Eddie, they were for my soul boiling over with hate and revenge. We had to move on, even if only for the sake of honoring Eddie…

*****

Black had spent the night in the guest house. At six o'clock in the morning we loaded up the limo and set out for the city. Black rolled two blunts and passed me one of them. We had to get our heads right for what lied ahead. Finally, breaking the silence between us, Black looked at me and said. "This time, my nucca, don't hesitate."

I knew exactly what Black was talking about. He was like my brother, he knew certain things about me that the average person could never detect. My hesitation had cost Eddie his life, and Nick sitting in jail. We pulled across the street from Fredrick Douglas School of Performing Arts. I told the driver to leave the engine running. It was only 7:20, we still had another 40 or 50 minutes before kids started showing up, which is why we got there early. Dressed in all black, together Black and I exited the limo crossing the street. We hastily walked around the playground to the teachers' parking lot. There were only a few cars in the lot, when an older white man pulled in. We watched the man park his Toyota, Corrolla near the staff entrance, he got out briefcase in hand and stepped inside the school. Never once did I see him fiddle with any keys, he just pulled the door open.

Assuming that the door was unlocked, I decided that would be our entrance. Black and I fell into step, hastily walking through the lot, reaching the door I pulled back the handle and scanned the long empty hallway. Black and I sneaked into the school. We hit rocks, then split up, each heading for our position. I was positioned in the janitor's closet on the third floor, right across from room 102, which is lil' Tavon's homeroom class.

I stood in the darkness of the closet, hand inside the sliding pocket of my hoody. I was massaging the butt of my 9 mm Berretta. "It won't be long," I quietly said, I was envisioning me standing over Amanda with the barrel of my gun poking her in the side of the head, while she pleaded for her life. "Won't be long…." I said.

Ding… Ding… Ding… The school bell sounded. Beep! Beep! Beep! My pager went off. It was Jackie hitting me 411. That was the code to let me know she was moving into position. I peeped out the crack of the door, and watched as the hallways filled with kids. They were laughing, some telling yo' moma jokes. The kids were me, Black, Rome, Lil' Pimp, and Rocko… Where'd the time go?...

Ding… The school bell brought me back to reality. My eyes locked on lil' Tavon as he entered the class room across from me. Seconds later, an agent walked into the classroom. I screwed the silencer onto the nose of my Berretta and waited. About twenty minutes later, the school's intercom crackled as a woman's voice came across. "Will Agent Loweskie, please report to the main office, you have a phone call." The intercom crackled, then buzzed off. That was the agent Black was responsible for. He was to take him out.

Agent Loweskie stepped into the hallway, and pulled his radio from his hip. It wasn't like the bureau to place a call like that. The fact that his cover was semi-blown just didn't sit right with him. He raised the Motorola two-way to his mouth and was about to speak into the receiver, but his eyes locked on the man standing before him.

Agent Loweskie lowered his radio to his side, and pleaded for mercy. "Please don't kill me. I have a wife and family waiting for me to get home," said Loweskie.

Black kept his distance from the agent. He didn't want to chance Loweskie reaching for the gun.

"Shut up," said Black through the clenched teeth. "Drop the radio on the floor and kick it over to me," order Black.

"That's it, nice and easy."

Loweskie gently kneeled down, setting his radio on the floor, then stood up slow.

"Kick it over," ordered Black.

Loweskie knew that it was now or never. He kicked the radio with his left foot. Timing it just right, he watched as Black's eyes lowered to the floor, locking on the sliding radio. Agent Loweski came from his right side pulling his

Glock from its holster. The swift movement of Loweskie raised Black's attention. Fhhh! Fhhh! Fhhh! Black squeezed off three shots into Loweskie's chest, sending him crashing to the floor. The silencer on Black's Beretta had muffled the shots. He stood over Loweskie who was trying to roll onto his side. Black reached down and picked up Loweskie's gun, then put it in his waist. He knew that he couldn't kill him in the hallway, because of the blood.

"Please don't kill me," said Loweskie, rolling onto his back and staring up the hole of the silencer. He wasn't hit, he was wearing a vest. The impact from the bullets just knocked the wind out of him.

"I'm not going to kill you. Get up," said Black. He stood back while Loweskie struggled to his feet.

"Walk," ordered Black, with the barrel of his gun. "In there," said Black. He was motioning Loweskie for the closet. But Loweskie turned around stopping short of the door. "Please don't kill me," pleaded Loweskie. He was now in tears.

"I told you that I wasn't going to kill you, now get in there," ordered Black.

Agent Loweskie reluctantly turned and stepped inside the closet. No sooner did he step through the door frame, Black pumped two slugs into the back of Loweskie's dome. His body slumped to the ground, and Black stood over it.

"I lied," said Black, then squeezed two more shots off. Fhh! Fhh!...

My watch sounded, marking the timer I had set. The school's intercom crackled and the secretary came over the loud speaker.

"Will Agent Mesharry, please report to the main office. You have a phone call," the intercom crackled, then buzzed off.

I was hunched over peering through the crack of the mop closet door. I intensely watched as the agent stepped to the front of the classroom, he said something to the teacher. She nodded, then he headed for the door.

I gripped the handle of my 9 mm. As soon as the agent stepped into the hall, I was on him. Fhh! Fhh! I planted two slugs into the agent's right knee sending him to the floor. Standing over him with the barrel of my gun pressed down into his scalp. "I'm not for any games, hear me?"

"Yes.." the agent cried. He was nursing his knee cap.

I reached into his jacket and disarmed him, pulling his Glock from his holster. I stuffed the gun into the back of my pants, then slapped the young agent in the back of the head with the butt of my gun. His face hit the floor hard. He was knocked out cold. Grabbing him by the feet, I dragged him into the janitor's closet from which I sprung. I pumped six slugs into the side of his face and watched as the holes opened up, and blood rose to the top, spilling over like lava from an erupting volcano. Blood was smeared in the hallway leading to the closet. I grabbed a mop, ran it under some hot water, and cleaned up the blood. I closed the door to the closet and took the stairs down to the staff entrance. I slid out of the school into the parking lot and threw my hoody on. I looked at my watch as I headed for my limo. Everything was going according to plan. I climbed inside the limo and hit rocks with Black who was already in the limo.

Chapter Thirty

It was 2:30 in the afternoon. Jackie had come through in the clutch. Against her better judgment, I had convinced her to help me in this. It was my way of testing her to see if in the face of fury, she would strap up and put it all on the line for her man. So far, Jackie had not let me down. I smiled at the sight of her exiting the front door of Fredrick Douglas. She was holding lil' Julian in one hand and lil' Tavon in the other. I had her pose as a social worker from Child Protective Services. She told the school that the mother had been reported for neglect. Jackie left a note with the secretary bearing an alias name and phone number for the secretary to give Amanda.

"That's right, baby handle business," I said from the back of the limo. The fact that Jackie was white made it easy for her to pull the boys from school without raising suspicion. She packed the boys into the backseat of the rental car, and then sped off.

Black and I hit rocks. "Hell, yeah!" I yelled. I poured Black and myself a glass of Crown Royal, then told the driver to pull around the corner.

*****

The secretary braced herself for a lashing, as she looked up to see Amanda stepping into the main office. The secretary stood to her feet, then walked around the counter to greet Amanda.

"How are you?" asked Amanda, smiling.

The secretary didn't return Amanda's smile. She reached out her hand, taking Amanda's. She ushered Amanda to the wooden bench in front of the counter and sat her down.

"Is something wrong?" asked Amanda, fearing what she thought to be the worst. Maybe one of her boys got hurt, she thought.

"Child Protective Services took your boys," said the secretary.

"What? Amanda jumped to her feet. "There has to be a mix up. What do you mean they took my boys, took them where? Where did they take 'em?" Amanda demanded.

"I'm sure it is a mix up, honey. The woman who took the boys left this for you." The secretary handed Amanda the note which Jackie had left.

"Can I use your phone?" asked Amanda, after reading the note.

"Sure, it's right there," said the secretary.

Amanda reached over the counter and picked up the receiver to the phone. She dialed the number on the note, and tapped her foot nervously as the phone began ringing…

*****

I looked at Black, then smiled as the car phone in the limo came to life. Ring… Ring… I picked up on the second ring, and held the phone to my ear without asking who it was. I listened intensely to Amanda's heavy breathing.

"Is this Child Protective Services?" asked Amanda.

I didn't say a work…

"Hello!" yelled Amanda. "Is this Child…"

"Nah, bitch- it's Satan…" I said.

I could tell by the slight pause that Amanda recognized my voice. "Oh, my God! Coach, please tell me you don't have my boys?" asked Amanda.

"Look, bitch, if you want to ever see them little rug rats again, you'll do exactly as I say," I said.

"Anything, Coach. Just don't hurt 'em, please. What do you want me to do?"

"I want you to first take a deep breath and regain your composure… Now, you're going to hang up the phone and meet a friend of mine. When you hang up, you're going to leave the school through the staff exit, it's to the left of the

main office. You can't miss it. You have one minute."
Click.

*****

Amanda nervously hung up the phone.
"Is everything okay, honey?" asked the secretary.
"Yeah, everything's fine. Thank you for letting me use the phone," said Amanda.
"No problem. Hope to see you tomorrow," the secretary said, as Amanda left out the office. Little did she know Amanda was praying the same thing.

Amanda took to her left down the hall. She pushed open the staff door and stepped into the parking lot. She stood there for a few moments looking around but saw no one.

Out of nowhere, Black wrapped his hand around her face, covering her mouth. "Shh..." he whispered into Amanda's ear. He nudged her in the lower back with the barrel of his gun, and together they began walking toward the curb.
"Pull up," I ordered the driver.
The limo met Black and Amanda at the curb of the street. I reached over and unlocked the door. Black opened the door, and shoved Amanda inside. He climbed in behind her

and the driver sped off. We turned down Grand Boulevard to see the agents still parked outside the school.

"Where are they, Coach?" demanded Amanda.

"Bitch!" I reached across and slapped the cowboy shit out of Amanda. "You don't know how long I've been holding that in," I said...

Amanda sat up in her seat. Her lip was split on the corner, and blood was starting to trickle down to her chin onto her blouse.

"You rat bitch, I shoulda' killed your ass long time ago. Because of you, two of my men are no longer with me. But we're going to fix that right now," I said raising my 9 mm to Amanda's head.

"You want your son to grow up without his father and mother? Go ahead, and kill me," said Amanda.

"Bitch, what the fuck are you talkin' 'bout, my son?" I asked.

"In case you didn't know. Tavon is your son. That's why he has your last name. All you gotta do is add up the months from the time you got locked up. I had Tavon six months after you went to jail..."

"That bitch is lying...." said Black...

Stay tuned for Part III

The Demise

After Chasin' Satisfaction, Julius finds that satisfaction is not all that it's cracked up to be. It left nothing but death in its aftermath. Now living the glamorous life in Miami while putting the finishing touches on his hybrid condo hotel, he realizes with newfound success he's now become the hunted. Julian's success is threatened as someone from his past vows revenge on him.

In Stores!!!

It may not be Histeria Lane, but these desperate housewives are fed up with their neglecting husbands. Their sexual needs take precedence over the millions of dollars their husbands bring home every year to keep them happy in their affluent neighborhood. While their husbands claim to be hard at work, these wives are doing a little work of their own with the bedroom bandit. Is the bandit swift enough to evade these angry husbands?

In Stores!!

NEGLECTED SOULS

Motherhood and the trials of loving too hard and not enough frame this story...The realism of these characters will bring tears to your spirit as you discover the hero in the villain you never saw coming...

In Stores!!!

Jimmy and Nina continue to feel a void in their lives because they haven't a clue about their genealogical make-up. Jimmy falls victims to a life threatening illness and only the right organ donor can save his life. Will the donor be the bridge to reconnect Jimmy and Nina to their biological family? Will Nina be the strength for her brother in his time of need? Will they ever find out what really happened to their mother?

In Stores!!!

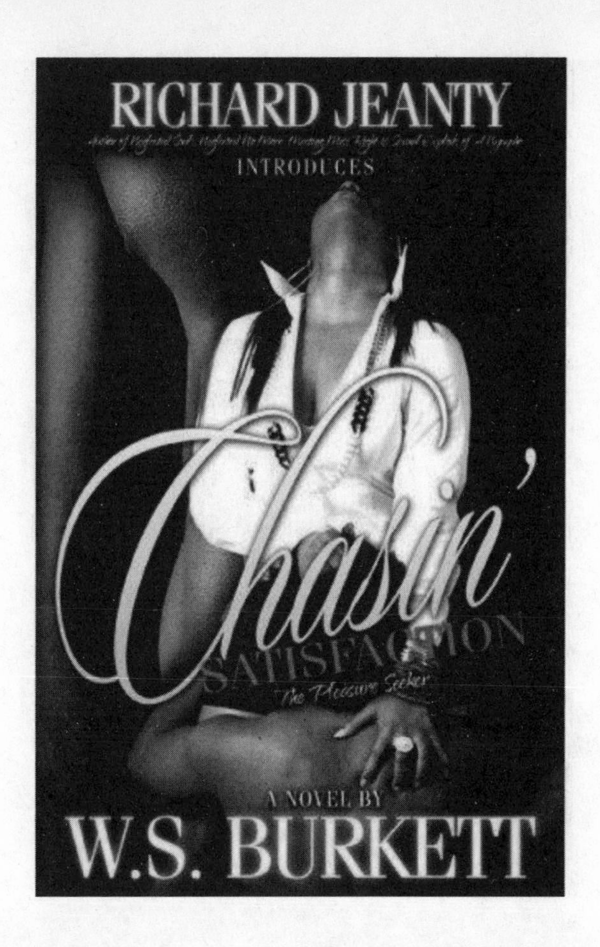

Betrayal, lust, lies, murder, deception, sex and tainted love frame this story... Julian Stevens lacks the ambition and freak ability that Miko looks for in a man, but she married him despite his flaws to spite an ex-boyfriend. When Miko least expects it, the old boyfriend shows up and ready to sweep her off her feet again. She wants to have her cake and eat it too. While Miko's doing her own thing, Julian is determined to become everything Miko ever wanted in a man and more, but will he go to extreme lengths to prove he's worthy of Miko's love? Julian Stevens soon finds out that he's capable of being more than he could ever imagine as he embarks on a journey that will change his life forever.

In Stores!!!

The police in New York and other major cities around the country are increasingly victimizing black men. The violence has escalated to deadly force, most of the time without justification. In this controversial book, noted author Richard Jeanty, tackles the problem of police brutality and the unfair treatment of Black men at the hands of police in New York City and the rest of the country.

In Stores!!!

Just when Darren thinks his relationship with Tina is flourishing, there is yet another hurdle on the road hindering their bliss. Tina saw a therapist for months to deal with her sexual addiction, but now Darren is wondering if she was ever treated completely. Darren has not been taking care of home and Tina's frustrated and agrees to a break-up with Darren. Will Darren lose Tina for good? Will Tina ever realize that Darren is the best man for her?

In Stores!!

Ronald Murphy was a player all his life until he and his best friend, Myles, met the women of their dreams during a brief vacation in South Beach, Florida. Sexual Jeopardy is story of trust, betrayal, forgiveness, friendship and hope.

In Stores!!!

Tina develops an insatiable sexual appetite very early in life. She only loves her boyfriend, Darren, but he's too far away in college to satisfy her sexual needs.
Tina decides to get buck wild away in college
Will her sexual trysts jeopardize the lives of the men in her life?

In Stores!!!

Faith Jones, a woman in her mid-thirties, has given up on ever finding love again until she met her son's best friend, Darius. Faith Jones is walking a thin line of betrayal against her son for the love of Darius. Will Faith allow her emotions to outweigh her common sense?

In Stores!!!

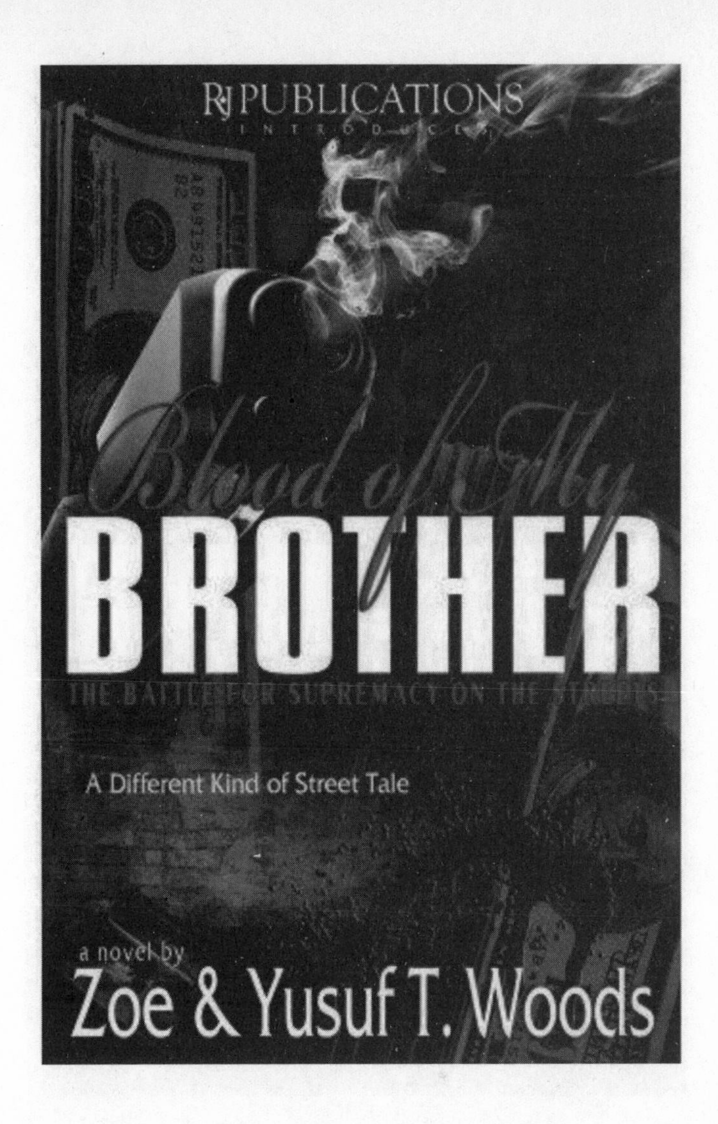

Roc was the man on the streets of Philadelphia, until his younger brother decided it was time to become his own man by wreaking havoc on Roc's crew without any regards for the blood relation they share. Drug, murder, mayhem and the pursuit of happiness can lead to deadly consequences. This story can only be told by a person who has lived it.

In Stores!!!

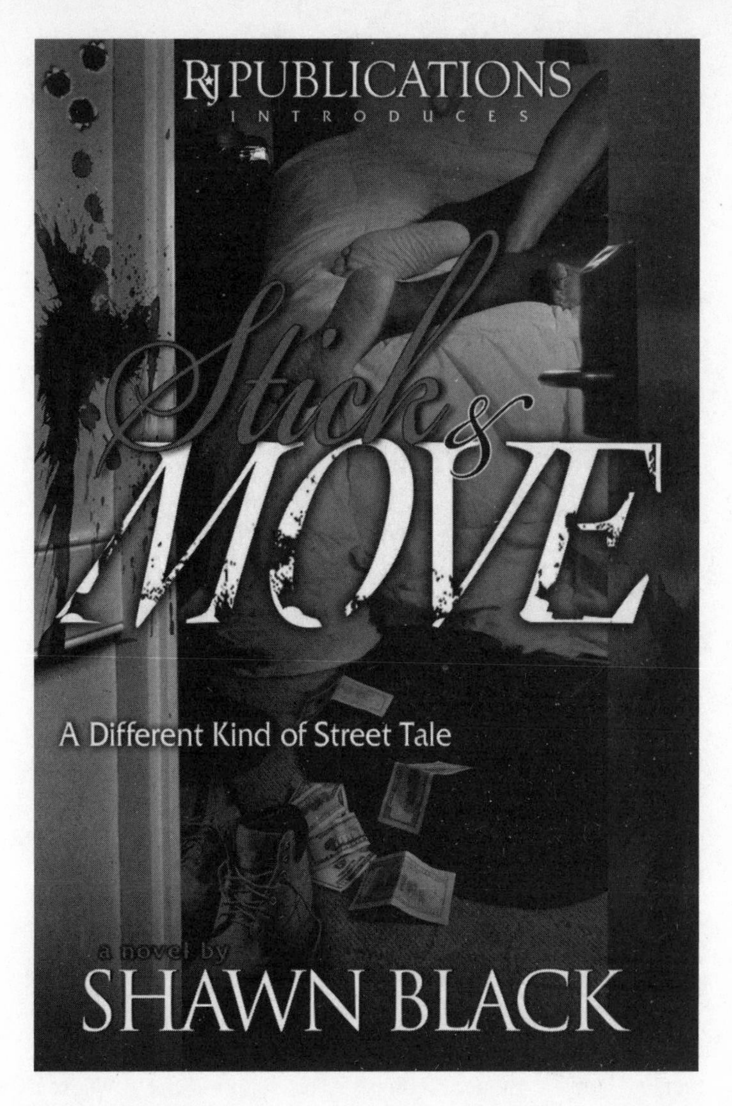

Yasmina witnessed the brutal murder of her parents at a young age at the hand of a drug dealer. This event stained her mind and upbringing as a result. Will Yamina's life come full circle with her past? Find out as Yasmina's crew, The Platinum Chicks, set out to make a name for themselves on the street.

In stores!!

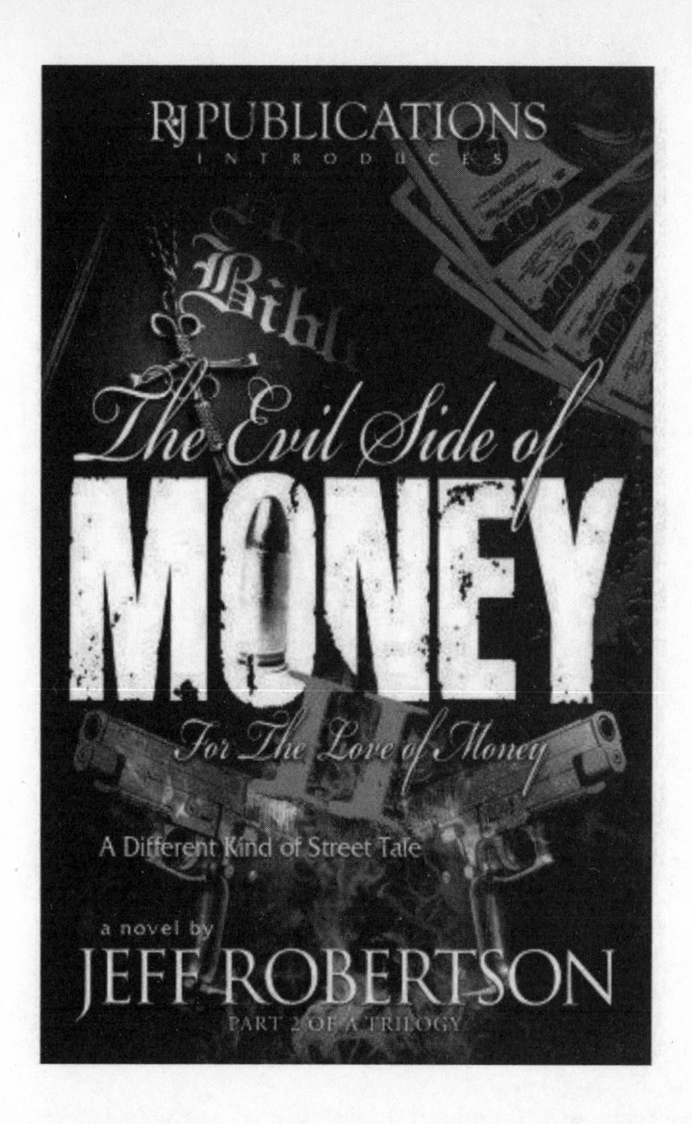

A beautigul woman from Bolivia threatens the existence of the drug empire that Nate and G have built. While Nate is head over heels for her, G can see right through her. As she brings on more conflict between the crew, G sets out to show Nate exactly who she is before she brings about their demise.

In Stores!!!

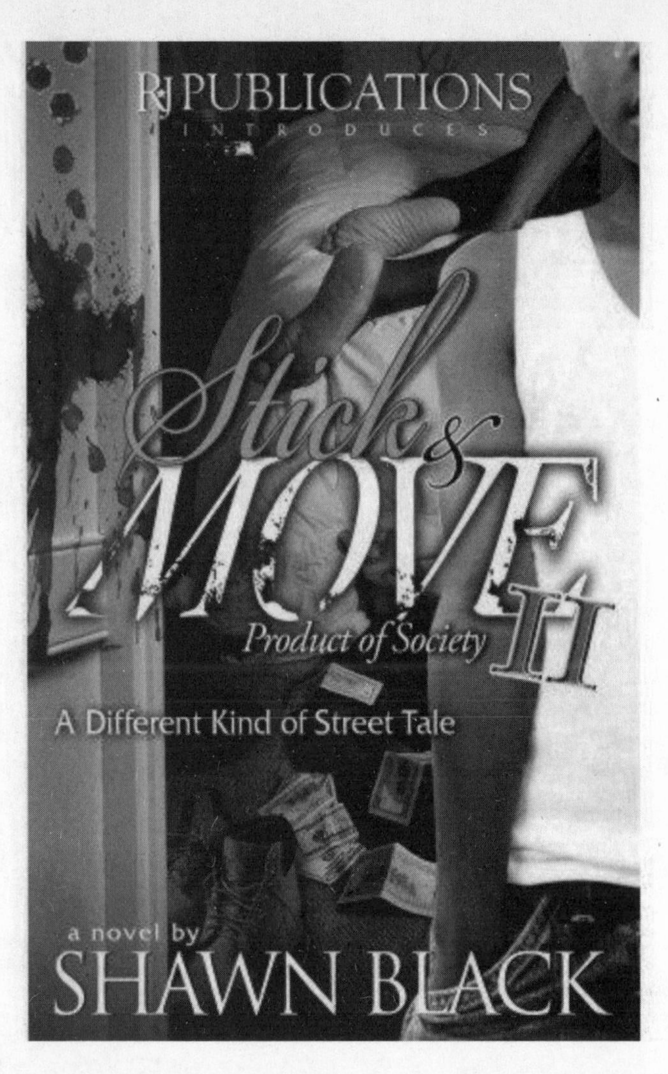

Scorcher and Yasmina's low key lifestyle was interrupted when they were taken down by the Feds, but their daughter, Serosa, was left to be raised by the foster care system. Will Serosa become a product of her environment or will she rise above it all? Her bloodline is undeniable, but will she be able to control it?

In Stores!!

An ex-drug dealer finds himself in a bind after he's caught by the Feds. He has to decide which is more important, his family or his loyalty to the game. As he fights hard to make a decision, those who helped him to the top fear the worse from him. Will he get the chance to tell the govt. whole story, or will someone get to him before he becomes a snitch?

In Stores!!!

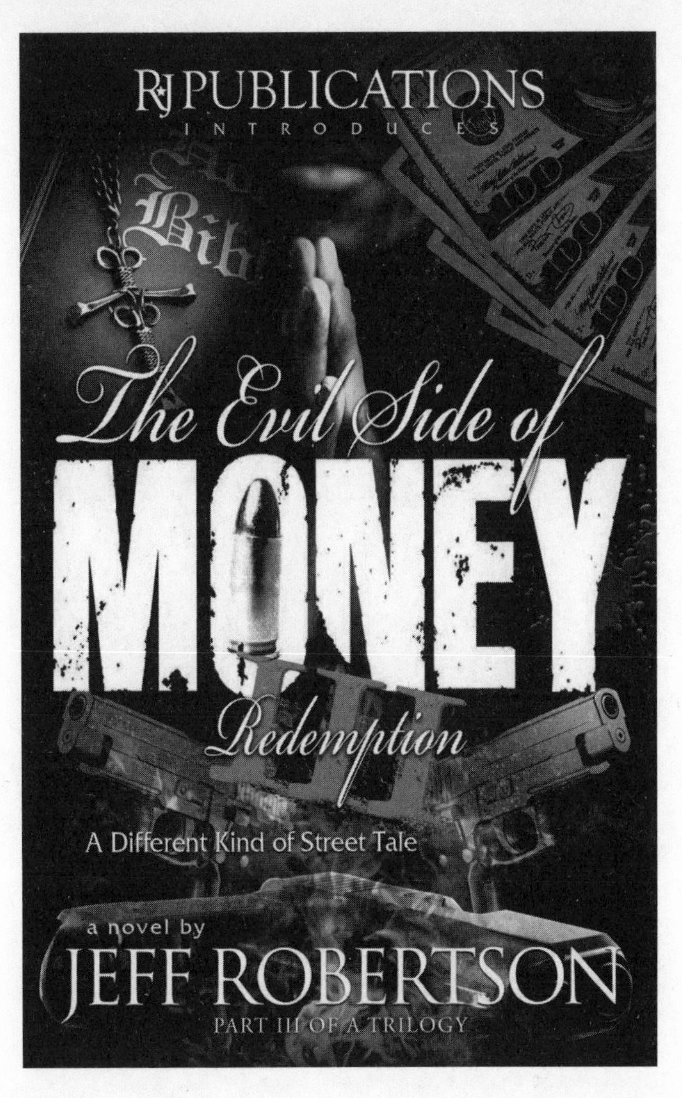

Forced to abandon the drug world for good, Nathan and G attempt to change their lives and move forward, but will their past come back to haunt them? This final installment will leave you speechless.

In Stores!!!

Nafiys Muhammad managed to beat the charges in court and was found innocent as a result. However, his criminal involvement is far from over. While Jerry Class Classon is feeling safe in the witness protection program, his family continues to endure even more pain. There will be many revelations as betrayal, sex scandal, corruption, and murder shape this story. No one will be left unscathed and everyone will pay the price for his/her involvement. Get ready for a rough ride as we revisit the Black Top Crew.

In Stores!!

Deon is at the mercy of a ruthless gang that kidnapped him. In a foreign land where he knows nothing about the culture, he has to use his survival instincts and his wit to outsmart his captors. Will the Hoodfellas show up in time to rescue Deon, or will Crazy D take over once again and fight an all out war by himself?

In Stores!!!

The drama continues as Deshun is hunted by Angela who still feels that ex-girlfriend Kayla is still trying to win his heart, though he brutally raped her. Angela will kill anyone who gets in her way, but is DeShun worth all the aggravation?

In Stores!!!

Buck Johnson was forced to make the best out of worst situation. He has witnessed the most cruel events in his life and it is those events who the man that he has become. Was the Johnson family ignorant souls through no fault of their own?

In Stores!!!

When an Ex-con finds himself destitute and in dire need of the basic necessities after he's released from prison, he turns to what he knows best, crime, but at what cost? Extortion, murder and mayhem drives him back to the top, but will he stay there?

In Stores !!!

RICHARD JEANTY
Author of Neglected Souls, Meeting Miss Right & Sexual Exploits of A Nympho
INTRODUCES
Insanely
IN
Love
WARNING
HIGHLY
ADDICTIVE
READING MATERIAL
A NOVEL BY
CEREKA COOK
Author of Extreme Circumstances

Pharaoh decides that his fate would not be settled in court by twelve jurors. His fate would be decided in blood, as he sets out to kill Tez, and those who snitched on him. Pharaoh s definition of Going All Out is either death or freedom. Prison is not an option. Will Pharoah impose his will on those snitches?

In Stores 10/30/2011

RJ
PUBLICATIONS
BRINGING EXCITEMENT, FUN AND JOY TO READING

RJ
PUBLICATIONS
BRINGING EXCITEMENT, FUN AND JOY TO READING